RAYYA DEEB

# SENECA

## EVOLUTION

THE SENECA SOCIETY BOOK III

RayyaDeeb.com



Happy Hedgehog
12400 Wilshire Blvd., Suite 1275
Los Angeles, CA 90025

ISBN: 978-1-7342016-3-5

Library of Congress Control Number: 2024926888

First Print, First Edition 2025

Cover Design by Chris Thompson/Lucky Ember Design

Explore Seneca

SenecaSociety.com

Happy Hedgehog

For Mom & Baba.

# 1

A VORTEX OF velvety vanilla light encircled me and unchained me from the constrictive restrictions of my earthly conditioning as teenage math genius, Doro Campbell. As I moved through the magnetic, glowing path I found myself no longer absorbed in anxieties stemming from my shattered family, questions of whom I could trust, or what unknown obstacles could lie ahead. I had been disentangled from the fears, tensions and chronic pains of life that had hardened deep in the tissues of my body.

My dear friend, Timothy Reba, had somehow found a way to guide me in this space beyond the body. Reba was beside me, his presence as certain as gravity itself. Reba wasn't just a friend; he was an Intuerian—a rare kind of being attuned to the subtle frequencies of existence. While most people wrestled with linear thoughts and tangible reality, Intuerians like Reba could effortlessly tap into layers of understanding that eluded the rest of us. They could sense connections, interpret the unseen, and move fluidly between the physical and metaphysical realms.

Here, in this space beyond my body, Reba's abilities were in full bloom. His spunky confidence wasn't just a personality quirk; it was the manifestation of his unique skill to navigate the currents of thought and energy, to guide those lost in the maze of their own fears.

*You're not alone, Campbella,* he said, his voice resonating. *You never were.*

That was Reba's gift—and his burden. As an Intuerian, he didn't just see the threads of destiny; he felt them like quantum vibrations resonating through his being.

Another small ball of light hovered with me, too, and even though all of this was seemingly new, it was as familiar as my childhood in Culver City.

A perfect pattern of connected, illuminated spheres formed the boundless ocean through which I effortlessly treaded. There was one hiccup in my tread though: my transfixion with the other ball of light. The closer I got to it, the less I saw that ball as separate from me, and then, just like that, with its blazing glow, we merged. All the stars in the galaxy blinked like a symphony. Thought ceased, and I became like a laser beam, blazing through the darkness in harmonic bliss with everything from the quarks and leptons, to the planets orbiting the sun and superclusters of flourishing universes far beyond any fathomable logic as far as the S.E.R.C. scholar in me was concerned.

*Now* was all that was. The clarified connectivity enabled me to tap into a universal language I hadn't yet known because I hadn't yet existed on a plane where such an understanding was possible. Or maybe I had been on it all along, but my racing mind propelled me into the extreme labyrinthine state of being human that situated my spot in a cloud of doubt. That cloud had evaporated in this flow. It seemed as though Reba, because he was Intuerian, had been capable of tapping into this landscape and brought me along. That must be why I had been so drawn to him from the moment we met on my first mind-blowing day deep inside the golden halls of Seneca. His presence grounded me. I wondered if all Intuerians, with their enhanced intuitive capabilities, existed in this wholly way; both inside and outside of their bodies.

With the fog gone and my mortal coil no longer holding me back, the core of me was free. My eyes weren't busy taking in images and processing data from the three dimensional world. This was a space where existing wasn't about tallying sights, sounds, and colors. Instead, I was a part of the infinite valley of wonder. I was the dirt and the sun and the stars but I was also swimming in an unseen expanse with temperatures colder than the polar ice caps and hotter than Death Valley. I had stress-induced hot feet no longer. Funny that although I had flat-lined and watched my heart stop, I felt more awake than ever. For the first time, I felt something more certain than the mathematics I once believed was the end-all-be-all. This *something* could not be translated into words or numbers. This something wasn't visible to my naked eye because it *was* the naked I. It was the Eye of the I.

My status was no longer ticking and tocking, but was instead being revealed as a continuum on which life and death ran its course. Eons of causes and effects played a role in landing me in this moment, from the tiniest of atoms to the formation of particles, to the dance of matter and antimatter annihilating one another over billions of years. As time slipped away, my entire being rippled outward into a sea of peace. The auto-pilot of my brain's programmed reality tunnel shut down and I was cradled in a warm bath of light.

I was empowered with a direct scope that let me see and feel the way the choices I had made in my life affected others. The warmth never went away as my eyes opened to the pain and sadness of people who lost their money in the gambling network I had hustled a couple years back. When I was fifteen I had written the algorithms to beat every gambling site in the world. Over two years I just saw the data and the numbers, not the *people* behind the millions of dollars my account had funneled into the Cayman Islands. I didn't think twice about the fact that thousands of people had put their money in to play an online game; a game that I had figured out how to code to my advantage. I didn't even care about the money, I just liked watching my clever home-made systems outsmart the ones put in place by global corporations from the United States to China. But what I had done was cheat the system, and my gain contributed to the pain of other people I did not know. Human beings. Not just the gamblers, but their families. Wives, husbands, parents, and kids. Sisters, brothers—I saw them all and how the impact reached deep into family trees. The despair that their gambling losses caused loved one upon loved one was an unbearable weight I never imagined would come back for me to hold with blood in my pale hands.

Truth wasn't all peachy and I'd written the playbook for my karma. It got heavier and heavier, and still there was more. Broken marriages, kids abandoned by shame-ridden parents. Global coding domination was not the win I thought it was. It was a lesson that every choice I made had a consequence, and I couldn't release the pressure of all this suffering yet because a powerful force awaited my arrival…

Along came Fatima. A girl who grew up in New Jersey. She loved pizza, soccer, and camping with her family, like I did with mine. She was fifteen when she was killed in a car accident on the Turnpike with her dad, Joe, who was driving completely obliterated on a Mojo Stick. Joe lost his family's savings and could never face real life from that moment forward. He began dabbling in Mojo Sticks to ease the pain of his failures. He took a second mortgage on their home and when the bank came to take that away, Joe didn't know where to turn. He saw how he had destroyed the life of his family and that wrecked him. He buried his reality under the extreme black haze of Mojo—which he might not have done if I hadn't created that rigged system to unfairly defeat an entire network of poker players. Thousands of them. Back when I did it I disregarded the players—it was their own fault for playing ball with me. Bucking the system was a cake walk, and I never once gave a thought about what was going down in the lives of the people playing the game. I never thought about Fatima, a girl like me, who lost her dad. She lost her family, and they, too, lost her. It was too late. I couldn't fix what I'd done.

I was hit with pangs of pain so deep and hard that my heart broke into thousands of tiny pieces, one for each person I hurt. It took a miracle shining through the cracks of the shattered glass to put it all back together. It took Fatima to rescue me—someone I hurt worse than I ever knew I could. She existed here in this space, too, beaming with forgiveness in her heart. She let me know that she didn't blame me for the way the cards were dealt in her lifetime. She told me she had moved on instead of holding on, and that was how she became free. Overwhelmed with the power of forgiveness this girl from New Jersey had for me, and for her dad, too, I was able to continue along on this extraordinary ride. As we traveled forward and backwards and sideways in time I realized my sheer significance in this infinite system, and Fatima's, too, and that every moment we created together would be inextricably linked, forever.

Reba led me along, soaring light years beyond the sky. We time-traveled through the awareness that my separateness from others was only an illusion. A realization that all that time I spent questioning the trust of the people around me was but the result of stories I had constructed in my head. It made sense that I couldn't find the truth I had been seeking because I was so blindly committed to the fiction.

It was hard not to want to remain embedded in this undulating plane of our collective origins, this blissed-out gleaming disk that sliced through the absence of light. But I felt a tsunami of a force come pluck me from this place and thrust me through dimensions. I rode it like a wave on Zuma straight to the shore. My body still had a purpose on Earth. I had to return. This is why the planet's pull was undeniably magnetic for me. I was vacuumed straight back down to face an uncertain fate that I was set to embrace on the Pale Blue Dot. With a hollow pop, I found myself laying back.

# 2

I OPENED MY eyes. The buttermilk soft, yet particularly potent light jolted my system and I gasped for my first waking breath. Taking in the tang of sterile ozone, above me, a BioSync Array pulsed softly. It scanned my body, micro-lasers stitching data streams in real time: heart rate, neural activity, cellular repair status. Thin filaments of NeuroGel cradled my head, transmitting a soothing hum designed to calm my synapses. The ceiling above shimmered with a faint, holographic overlay displaying my vitals—an elegant ballet of graphs, numbers, and fractal patterns. Technology wasn't just fixing me; it was listening to me, adjusting to my needs with the precision of a quantum metronome.

My mouth, though, was arid like the Sahara. I exhaled through my nose and my sandpapery tongue pressed against the roof of my mouth. Chilled air streamed in through my bone-dry nostrils and puffed up my lungs. I held onto that air as if someone was about to snatch it away from me. Then I released it from my body. I wanted more. I breathed in deep again, this time less concerned that my breath could be swiped away from me. My ears tuned to the symphonic purrs and buzzes of machinery. Thought resurfaced, deciphering the insane notion that I'd just experienced a journey back into my body. Just hours ago—*or was it days?*—I'd been dangling between life and death.

I felt my mind and body reconnect, but this time I wouldn't let my thoughts run wild. I'd guide them. I acknowledged my physical place in this world and trillions more, as a finite chunk of organic mass, but I was also ingrained into a system beyond the reason and numeric data, and from this system, I was not separate. The power of this mysterious domain seemed to evaporate my all-consuming singular objective of grasping for answers and I felt at peace. It had occurred to me that answers to equations, if I was to find them, could only satisfy me temporarily.

All I wanted was to see my mom's face and hug her. She had always been there, forgiving me despite my screw-ups. I had to make sure that she knew that I was okay and I was here for her. I'd drifted too far away from her in my drive to bring justice to Seneca. The fixation I had on finding my dad in South America was a burden because my mom was the one person that loved me unconditionally and she was always there right in front of me. Whether I slacked in school, or when I got busted hot-hacking a flighter for a joy ride with Julie, my mom always forgave me.

Even though nobody around me was cognizant that I had opened my eyes, I felt an overwhelming sense of their presence. Their minds were pushed to full-throttle, fussing with stats and tasks to bring me back. They were too busy to notice that I had arrived. Their desire to save me radiated love like rays of the sun. The warmth lifted my spirits. It didn't take eyes to realize these connections of ours were electric—I felt it in my core.

I shifted my eyes to look down at the shape of my body under a crisp white sheet. I moved my stiff toes and the corners of my mouth lifted to the heavens as if being puppeteered by the ultimate force in all of the universe. This body was my vessel for experiencing life, yet it also reinforced the illusion of separateness. Not anymore… Not anymore.

My thinking and questioning kicked back in with a heavy sense of wonder about where I was. I recalled where I had been before I took a spin off the grid. My eyes shifted in their sockets to take in my surroundings: The metallic, plastic, rubber, and cement structures that composed the room I was in emitted lights, sounds, and vibrations. People moving throughout it all with vision and dedication. I knew I was here again—in the glorious, technologically incomparable, chiseled-out world, oozing with possibility, beneath the surface of the earth: Seneca. While at one point I couldn't fathom living underground, below the earthworms and dirt, this depth was my present now and everything was illuminated.

I tried to sit up, and the sensors erupted in a frenzy. In seconds I was surrounded by physicians, assistants, and my mom, Layla Campbell. She pushed her way up from behind them all, and jeez, did she look beautiful. Her face was everything in that moment. Her forehead tight, clenched jaw, fatigued eyes—the entirety of her expression painted a clear picture for me of her pained recent days and extreme discomfort in the uncertainty of what was happening to me. Every inch of her was covered in distress, from untamed hair tossed up in a knot, to her feet that shuffled nervously on the ground. In an instant the tension subsided as her eyes filled with joy by catching the life that had returned to mine. I hadn't felt this level of relief to see her since I was a little girl crying after a nightmare and she came to comfort me. I had little-to-no-concern for the action that was going on around me; physicians checking monitors and asking questions that I couldn't quite form words to answer.

I watched my mom closely. Without knowing how long I had been out of my body, but just by seeing through the lens of her demeanor, I understood how long she had been waiting for me to come to. My gut sank like an anchor in the deep blue sea. I knew I couldn't take back how I had made my mom feel, but I *could* move forward with a greater responsibility for her well-being. As I looked about the room, it really sank in that everyone here was someone's mother, father, brother, sister, son or daughter. We *all* had this responsibility to each other.

I had to get my bearings straight. I wanted to know what day it was. I tried to dive into my Veil via my flex implant, but it was totally unresponsive. Normally, with this computational implant of mine, I could access the super-grid of data which contained everything from personal health statistics to my contacts, and everything in between and beyond. Perhaps it was my newly awakened state that I needed to adapt to in order to get back on the grid. I tried to pull up my Veil again, even harder this time. It was no wonder it didn't work. I'd asked my mind to power up just after it had been commanded to take a backseat. Mixed signals. And maybe, deep down, I wasn't sure I wanted it back online.

The flex implant had been a lifeline—my tether to information, people, and places I couldn't otherwise reach. But it was also a shackle. A silent, unblinking eye watching from the shadows. I longed for normalcy, for a reality where my thoughts were my own and my decisions weren't tangled in the web of encrypted networks and unseen eyes.

My fingers hovered near my temple, feeling the faint pulse beneath the skin, knowing that my flex lay dormant inside my body. For a moment, I hesitated. Disconnected, I was vulnerable... but free. And yet, in the quiet space beyond the data streams, something settled deep within me.

I had everything I needed.

"Mom," I muttered.

"Doro," she gasped as she leaned down and tucked her arms up under mine.

I was alive.

# 3

A HALF-DOZEN doctors and assistants tried to block my mom, but she held her ground, clutching the cot with one hand and caressing my arm with the other. My mom's affection kept me stable. As my eyes traveled from one doctor to another and another, I felt increasingly vulnerable. I didn't want to be on this cot, under anyone's watch.

I recognized pearly, gray-haired Dr. Cairncross standing shoulder to shoulder with my mom. She commanded the room with poised authority, taking data and giving instructions in calm, swift motions. She turned her attention to me. "Dorothy Campbell, do you know where you are?"

"Claytor Lake," I asserted.

Dr. Cairncross's chin dropped, her eyes closed, and she released a guttural sigh of relief. She lifted her head, straightened herself and I think I saw a smidgen of a smile. "Yes. We are in the Center for Quantum Neurology and Consciousness

Experimentations, and I am Dr. Renee Cairncross. Do you remember me, and this place?"

"Mm hm."

"We are all so relieved that you are back," she said, with a softer tone than what I remembered ever coming from her. In my past interaction with Dr. Cairncross she was all business and devoid of emotion.

As a determined physician shined a laser light in my eye, Dr. Cairncross spoke to me, "I was working with you on an experimental neurological technique when your neurotransmitters went erratic and your body went into cardiac arrest. Can you feel your toes?"

"Yes."

"And do you know who this is?" She looked to my mom and gestured a hand towards her.

As my eyes fell on my mom a soothing vibe washed over me, and I gently nodded.

"I love you, Doro," my mom whispered, her voice trembling with sorrow and relief. It was the shake in her voice that planted me solidly back on this plane, in this room, right here, right now. *She* was the gleaming disk of light. The sunlight that revived my wilted petals.

"I'm sorry, Mom. I'm so sorry."

My mom dropped her her cheek to my chest and through stifled cries she whispered, "No guilt right now, my sweet girl.

You are here. That's all that matters."

I held her head against my beating heart. The strong whiff of coffee from her hair and rose water on her skin warmed me up even more. The familiarity seeped in deep and calmed me. I was home. We didn't want to let go of each other. But then I felt the hole we needed to fill.

"Where's Dad?" I whispered.

My mom pulled back a few inches, trying to mask a peculiar look. "Doro?"

"Where is he?"

"Hon, Dad's been gone for almost four years."

I shook my head, "I saw him."

Then it hit me and I was floored by the reminder that my mom didn't know my dad was still alive. Memories flooded back —sneaking to South America, finding Dad, almost dying in the jungle. This torrential memory avalanche resurrected unwelcome anxiety and exhilaration. I had to catch my own breath. My mom had no idea I had seen my dad in South America, and she couldn't know. Not yet.

"You've been unconscious for fifty-four days," Dr. Cairncross said, dropping back into default monotone mode.

I peered up at Dr. Cairncross, crinkling my eyebrows in disbelief. Fifty-four days was insane. It couldn't have been. My mom stood back up and I turned to her for verification. *Fifty-four days?* I asked with my eyes and my eyes alone. I could tell by the tightness in her face and her sudden forced, erect posture that she was trying to be strong for me, but she couldn't hold back the tears or hide the fears that emanated from her. She dabbed her nose with a tissue hidden in her fist.

"But, I, I, I—this doesn't, it doesn't make sense." I couldn't help but stutter because my mind was churning and trying to grasp facts that were nowhere to be found.

"It's okay," my mom whispered, "you're okay." But the tiny throbbing vein on her temple and welling-up eyes didn't say I was okay. I received her body language as a warning signal even if that wasn't her intention.

The amount of time didn't add up. I became aware of my confusion and I slowed down, not allowing it to overtake the rich core of me I had just traversed into. That part of me suddenly spoke up, urging me to stay awake—not to just kick back and catch the fragments of information hurled my way.

"Where is Reba?" I asked, Dr. Cairncross.

"Who?"

"My friend, Reba. He was with me—"

"Nobody named Reba was ever here," she assured me.

"He absolutely was." I was equally as sure, if not more.

My mom looked at Dr. Cairncross with a slightly tilted head.

"Ms. Campbell, near-death experiences can blur reality and imagination—"

"I need to see him."

"I'm afraid I don't have the authority to bring him here."

"Ellen Malone. Ellen! Where is Ellen?"

"One of my assistants has been in touch with her. She is on her way."

That wasn't good enough. I sat up and inspected my body and all the monitors. Digital. Robotic. Data beyond the scope of my repertoire.

My mom put her hand on my arm, "Doro, just take it easy."

"Mom, I *need* to talk to Reba."

"I know, hon, and you can. Soon—"

"Now. I need him *now*."

I started to peel the monitors off my body. Dr. Cairncross watched me, disapprovingly. "Not a good decision, Ms. Campbell. You know your mother and I both have your best interest in mind, but if you do things like this we won't be able to help you."

"Doro, please don't do this—" my mom urged.

"Mom, I love you to death. I'm sorry you've been put through hell with me, but I'm nobody's guinea pig. I need to speak with Reba and Ellen and until I say so *nobody* touches me."

My mom's tight shoulders suddenly relaxed, and rather than trying to convince me of anything I needed or need not do, she became quiet. She let my message sink in. As we stared into each other's eyes, I felt her tuning into my intuition and settling into her own, trusting in this unseen place above that of the sophisticated system of people and computers surrounding us. The unwavering love and trust we shared drowned out the noise. She turned to Dr. Cairncross, "We will wait for Ellen."

Although Dr. Cairncross came with science as her sword, she was not lacking in the consciousness department. She dipped her head and benignly nodded, "Very well."

As the adrenaline in me began to subside I crashed back onto my cot. My body was too weak to sit up.

After a half hour of silence, "Doro, thank god!" I heard and lifted my heavy eyelids to see Ellen rushing in. It was rare to get anything other than cool from Ellen's trademark composure, but when I did, I knew it was real. From the moment we met when she recruited me to The Seneca Society, I had been captivated by her intelligence, her power, and the mysterious motivations that surrounded her. Now, though, instead of allowing my mind to attempt to define her, my heart was fully present.

"Ellen, I'm so glad you're here."

"Of course I'm here. I came as soon as I heard you were back," she said with a tremble I'd only heard once before when she told me about leaving her son, Connor, behind in the Aboves. For a moment her words were lost on me because I was taken by what was wrapped inside that tremble—Ellen's love for me. I knew that she would get that what I was asking for was something I truly needed. "Nobody understands," I said to her. "Please. I need to see Reba."

She nodded, "Okay. I will do my best to make that happen, but first we need to ensure that you're stable."

"I am."

"We need clearance from Dr. Cairncross. We are absolutely not taking another chance," Ellen insisted. Ellen had the sort of discernment to know that even if my heart was on solid ground, I needed my body in proper working order, too. I couldn't disagree, but patience was still an elusive virtue for me.

My mom lunged forward like a lioness towards Ellen. "No chance she leaves here without medical clearance. And even then, I'm not letting her out of my sight until *I* know she's okay."

"I understand your concern—"

"Oh, do you?"

My mom and Ellen shared a wicked stare down and I saw something intense brewing. It was unusual. Dense. Familiar. Like there was history between them. My mom's lip shook and she spoke piercingly to Ellen, "No mother would ever sacrifice her child as a pawn for information."

Ellen's eyes shifted to hit every individual in the room before she moved in close to my mom, staring her dead in the eye and scorchingly said, "A few years in a coffee shop and you've forgotten your oath."

Oath? What the heck *oath* was Ellen talking about? My mom became flustered for just a fraction more than a split second but she gathered herself just as quickly and looked back to me. Everything was starting to become confusing again and I desperately didn't want the fog to return.

"Where is Reba?" I asked Ellen, whose eyes were still pinned to my mom.

"The last I saw him was when we left your residence to come here," Ellen said. "I've been told he's working on an Intuerian project in the Aboves—"

"Wait, he's in the Aboves? That's impossible."

The room seemed to tilt as my mind raced. Reba? In the Aboves? It made no sense. He wouldn't leave me—not after everything we'd been through. "Why would he go there? He didn't even say goodbye."

"Some things aren't meant to be shared, Doro."

It was all coming back to me: Ellen, Reba, Dom and myself were all together just before I found myself here. I was in my residence replanting deleted memories into my brain from a back-up. I had become increasingly delirious in the process, and my body was hardcore crashing. Reba came to my room, and then Dom. There was an argument. Next thing I remember was being submerged in saline… and then bam, here I am.

"And Dom?" I asked.

"He's in session." Ellen said.

"Can I see him?"

"Soon."

My mom stepped towards me and added, "Doro, he has been by your side every single morning before session and again after session until after dark, for *fifty-four days*."

As I lay there I felt lifted as if butterflies were pulling me up by strings. Dominic Ambrosia—our hearts collided in this techno playground, but I knew our bond ran deeper than this place. It might have felt like a bond that only formed in S.E.R.C.'s golden halls, but what I was realizing was that we could have very well been connected for long before we were even born.

Ellen's face softened and her eyes squinted, "I know I warned you about Dominic when you first came here, but I was wrong. I've never seen such dedication as he's shown to you. He eats his dinner on the acoustic carrier as he travels to see you after his sessions, *every single day*."

"I can't believe I did this to him. I can't believe I did this to all of you."

Ellen shook her head.

My mom bent down next to me and pressed her warm, clammy cheek to mine. "Doro, do not for one second blame yourself for any of this. You couldn't have known. We never know what life will present us with. We take it in strides and we take it *together*, with faith that everything we do has a purpose."

For a moment we all stayed quiet. I closed my eyes and let my mom's resilience energize my crushed heart before the buzz of the lights pulled me back to the situation at hand.

"Ellen, I have to see him, now."

# 4

I BLINKED AWAKE to Becky Hudson, the girl-next-door B3 News correspondent, delivering Senecan hope over bleak footage of the Aboves; people in blazing sun and heat standing in sun suits and goggles, enduring never-ending lines to get into grocery stores. Inside, rationed goods distributed by downtrodden employees.

*"The decline of bee populations in the Aboves may prove irreversible, and as temperatures continue to rise, leading to prolonged droughts and storms of unparalleled magnitude that decimate entire counties of farmland, the complete depletion of Earth's food supply becomes only a matter of time. Fortunately, our very own bee-bot technology in Seneca has paved the way for a produce resurgence that we will take with us for a clean, health-forward slate on Mars."*

Footage of bee-bots pollinating underground crops cut to Senecans selecting vibrant, plump produce from abundant markets. It all looked enticing, almost too perfect, like a cartoon.

I was curled into a ball with my black, beefy-breath Pomeranian, Killer, cuddled up right next to my head in my mom's bed. I shut the monitor off. I must have slept for a week solid after I left inpatient rehabilitation at Claytor Lake and came to my mom's place in the Residence Sector. The days and nights seemed to blend together and the only reason I knew it was morning was because my mom came in with a tray of oatmeal and orange juice. "Morning, honey."

She sat next to me on the bed.

"You're the best mom ever."

"Aw. My sweet girl." She tucked my hair behind my ear. "Doro… you do realize," she took a deep breath, "at some point we need to talk about you going back to session."

"Can we not?" I pleaded, as I sat up and downed the glass of orange juice.

"It will be good for you to get out of this bed and back into a normal routine."

"Ugh." Routine felt like the real threat.

Killer repositioned himself into my lap.

"You're much healthier now, physically and mentally. I'm afraid if you spend too much time sleeping you'll go backwards."

"I'm just not ready to be back in the world. I don't even think that is what I want anymore."

"What, going to session?"

I nodded ever so slightly. There was a part of me that wanted to go back, but not to exactly how it was before.

"You still need to learn, Doro. So it's either session here in Seneca, or back to school in the Aboves—if you're prepared to go back. I do have to warn you, life back home is even worse off than it was when you saw it last."

"That's the kind of stuff I don't want in my head. Worrying about what's happening with the world. I just want to be here with you and Killer, doing normal teenager things. I feel like I lost that, and I'm exhausted."

I watched as the look of guilt washed over my mom with her sunken eyes. She tucked her chin to her chest and then turned to connect with my eyes.

"You're here now, Doro, and you're okay. I plan to make sure we keep it that way," my mom said as she rubbed my back. It was just the comfort I needed, but there was something I had been wondering about.

"Mom?"

"Yeah, hon?"

"What did Ellen mean by your *oath*?"

My mom closed her eyes. When she opened them she kept a stoic gaze and said, "One day we will talk more about the life dad and I had long ago, but for now, let's keep our focus off of stories of the past and on your wellness."

I knew my mom would talk when she was ready, and honestly, I was too exhausted to push—but something was clearly there. I nodded and hugged her. With a gentle certainty in her voice she said, "I know that going back out into the world after a traumatic experience like what you've been through isn't exactly easy, but I know you have it in you to rally. Believe me —from my own experience, the sooner you get back into normal life the sooner you can overcome this anxiety you're feeling. And I am one hundred percent positive there is a certain young man who is waiting there for you." She gave me a knowing smile, her eyes softening. "He made quite an impression on me, you know."

That warmed my heart. I lifted the spoon from the tray and took a little taste of the oatmeal. Wow. Whoever knew that oatmeal could be a transcendent experience?

My mom moved her hand to my shoulder and looked at me with her lips tucked in. Her concern plucked at the fibers of my body like strings on a stand up bass. There was something deeper going on in her head, but I couldn't begin to wrap my head around it. More than wanting to decipher her thoughts, more than absolutely anything, I wanted to squash her suffering. My mom had given her life to taking care of others. She had earned peace once and for all. "Okay. I get it. I'll go." I said, committed to her welfare above all else, but something compelled me to file a disclaimer. "But if I don't feel right, I'm coming back."

She smiled, "Deal."

Even though I didn't want to, a part of me was curious. I wondered if Dad's discovery of Doromium had made it into session rooms, or if the Mars colonization plans had shifted. Who was down with the Departers and wanting to abandon the Earth for a new life on Mars, versus who was on team Repairer, wanting to clean up our planet?

Once the questions started flowing in my head, I couldn't stop them. But more importantly than my endless stream of curiosities, I needed to see Dom and Reba, and that hadn't yet been possible, because Dr. Cairncross had deactivated my flex implant during my coma. I was hesitant about re-activating it. Off-the-grid living was peaceful. I still didn't have access to my Veil, but I didn't need it. The downside was that Dom and Reba didn't have access to my mom's residence. I was basically in isolation.

Without the flex implant activated, the world felt muted, like a song stripped of its melody. I now found my thoughts drifting aimlessly in the void. At first, it felt liberating—freedom from the network that tracked my every move. But now, that freedom felt suspiciously like being stranded, the quiet was more oppressive than peaceful. Every moment stretched longer, my mind hyperaware of the nothingness filling the space where connections once were.

I had always believed I was more than my flex connection. I pressed my fingers against my temple, as if I could will the dormant implant to come back to life. Nothing. Just skin. Just me.

I thought about how my mom had always told me I could handle anything, that I didn't need to depend on anyone—or anything—to survive. But she didn't understand this world, this system. She didn't know what it was like to exist on a grid where survival often depended on being faster, smarter, more connected than everyone else.

My breath hitched, a sudden surge of panic tightening my chest. Was this what normal felt like? Or was this what failure looked like? I pushed the thought aside, forcing myself to breathe slower, deeper. I didn't have the luxury of breaking down. If the flex wasn't going to guide me, I'd have to rely on the one thing I'd avoided for so long—myself.

It was terrifying.

And it was thrilling.

For the first time in as long as I could remember, there was no voice but my own. Maybe, just maybe, that was enough. And I knew one thing for sure, my mom was right: It probably was time to get back to real life.

I peeled myself out of my mom's bed and over to the bathroom. As I got ready, I tried to keep my anxieties at bay about going back out into the population of Senecans, who, like me, had also been recruited for their stellar acumen in fields ranging from technology to medicine and beyond. This was no ordinary secret society, and I was no ordinary girl. But I wanted a chance to be just that—a simple girl with a simple life. First, I wanted to see Dom and I knew he would be coming out of session.

# 5

Seneca's Education and Research Center (S.E.R.C.) was leagues beyond my high school in L.A. Here, sessions catered to our skills and interests, not some outdated curriculum. I stepped off the acoustic carrier into the hallway ablaze with scholarly enthusiasm. It felt jarring, yet refreshing to be back in the mix.

I now knew that the walls were alive in this corridor. PulseLines—thin veins of luminescent circuitry—ran along the edges, updating in real-time with the movements of everyone in the complex. In the distance, a group of scholars moved through a Quantum Archway, the system verified their identities at the molecular level. All this action around me, yet I was cut off—immersed in a world of seamless connectivity and suddenly feeling more alone than ever.

My pulse practically popped out of my skin as I stood in the intersection I knew Dom would cross through on his way in from the acoustic carrier stop that transported him from the youth residences to S.E.R.C. Or at least I thought he would be here, because this was how it almost always went in the past, but how did I really know that's how it would go at this moment? The past didn't guarantee the present or future.

My heart thumped faster and harder. I tapped my shoes on the pristine ground, anxiously awaiting Dom's return into my ether. It had been two whole months that we'd been apart. I know Dom had gotten word from Ellen that I was no longer in C-QNCE—Seneca's Center for Quantum Neurology and Consciousness Experimentations, and that I was recovering at my mom's place the past few days. Even though my mom had returned my flexer, I chose not to reach out until now. I wanted this moment—our reunion—to happen face to face.

My gaze flitted restlessly across the crowd, my breath catching every time someone vaguely resembled him. The anticipation was almost unbearable. I reeled my thoughts back in like a fishing line that had been cast far out into a lake. As they wound back up nice and neat, I felt the patter of my heart relaxing like the final raindrops after a storm. I dropped into a delicate breath, closed my eyes and held them shut as I popped thoughts away like ping pong balls. Nope. No thank you. Buh-bye.

When I opened my eyes they met Dom's. There he was, twenty yards away. He froze mid-stride. My smile reached from ear-to-ear. The field of bliss between us was everything and I was suddenly nowhere but in it.

Dom sprinted over. He didn't say a word, just lifted me, and kissed me. "You're here! I can't believe it!"

I laughed joyfully and squeezed my arms around him. My heart did somersaults.

"I missed you," I said, and I meant it more than ever. I kissed him again like I couldn't get enough, and the world stopped spinning. Dom pulled back and squinted as he looked questioningly at me, as if trying to register if I was actually really right in front of him.

"Doro, every day I was with you and—

"I know you were."

"It killed me seeing you like that, but I knew you'd come back. I just felt it."

"I felt it too."

"You did?"

"Yeah, it's something I don't think I'll ever be able to explain, but the best way I can put it is that even though it seemed like I was gone, I wasn't."

Dom pulled me in and held me tight again, "How can I go back to session now? I can't imagine focusing on work knowing you're back and we're not together."

We took each other in and I pondered the alternative to going our separate ways for the day.

"Then don't," I suggested.

Dom squinted and tilted his head. Dominic Ambrosia was at the top echelon of scholars in every single one of his sessions. He wasn't one to blow off academics, but I had to ask, "Just one day… me and you," I urged.

His wheels were spinning.

"God. I wish." He smiled.

"Come on then, let's do it. Nobody knows I'm supposed to be back in session yet and you can just call in sick or something." I couldn't let go of him. Not yet.

"They're everywhere now," he muttered, his voice just above a whisper.

I forced a smile, trying to shake the chill that settled over me. "Let them watch. We're not doing anything wrong."

But we both knew better. In Seneca, innocence was just a matter of perspective.

Dom pressed his lips together pensively as he pondered my suggestion. I loved being a bad influence on him. I was bright-eyed and bushy-tailed for the first time in eons and even though he shook his head *no*, he totally wanted to blow off his day for us to be together.

"I like how you think," he said with a grin.

"Ditto."

Dom looked around as if he was about to get away with something, and then back at me with a playful smirk. I slipped my hand into his and nodded my head down the hall. Without another word we dashed hand-in-hand to the acoustic carrier.

I sat in the nook under Dom's arm the whole ride back to my residence where we spent the day catching up and basking in each other's company. We made cups of ramen and sat in bed just talking and laughing and playing classic records; Foo Fighters and Endless Horizon. I missed my jams. Really, this was the first time we got to chill in peace and just be. Dom gave me a back rub and filled me in on some gossip from when I was in a coma. Who liked whom and all that stuff that didn't matter, but that's all I wanted to hear. It sure was easier on the ears than stories of global deception. Dom told me Jennifer Wallingsford's friend McKayla actually checked in on me while I was in the hospital, which I was shocked to hear, considering the hard time she gave me when I first arrived in Seneca. It was nice to think that McKayla actually had a heart underneath that porcupine layer.

"What about Jennifer?" I asked.

"I haven't seen her or her brother in weeks."

"That's weird."

"Everything is weird," Dom replied.

"True."

"Except you, Doro." He said as he yawned and laid down next to me. When we were together, time disintegrated and before we knew it, it was night. Laying there, forehead-to-forehead with Dom, I was transported to a realm of tranquility that felt familiar and safe. I didn't want to drift away from soaking up this magic. It was no wonder I could never get Dom out of my head when we were apart. Apparently, the heart doesn't let you decide when or where you think of the one you love—and it shouldn't, because this bliss was what it was all about.

In the featherbed of the quiet night I clung to the sweet sound of Dom's breath fading in and out. Our rhythms meshed. My chest tingled next to the warmth of his body. I didn't want to return to a world locked in hate, war, and greed. It was glaringly clear that when we became entangled in that mess outside of our cherished space our lives were suffocated.

Before I knew it, I had fallen asleep. That was a gift I would not take for granted. I was the queen of sleepless nights, after-all—a position I would gladly relinquish.

I'd been to hell and back during the disorienting mind hack I experienced out in the Peruvian wilderness when I was on the mission to find my dad in the South American Seneca City hub. My flex implant had been under siege by none other than Flex Technology Corporation and I realized that I had yet to reactivate it since the whole NeuroQue procedure that almost killed me. I'd undergone the procedure to trace the bug on my flex implant, but the process nearly destroyed me. When I tried to replant my memories manually, one-by-one, it made my brain go haywire, tailspin, and cause an entire system crash. I was fortunate enough to be at C-QNCE in the hands of one of the world's top quantum neurologists, Dr. Cairncross. She restored my virus-free brain with all of my memories and a disconnected flex implant so that I would no longer be vulnerable to such attacks. It was apparent there were rival factions that wanted control of my mind.

My flexer was my means to communicating with people far away from me, like my mom, yet I still hadn't the courage to kickstart it back into action. That hack didn't conquer me though. The corrupt and nefarious S.O.I.L. agent, Gregory Zaffron—who challenged the greater good with his selfish motives—could not destroy the bond Dom and I shared.

Dom, Reba and Ellen found me out in the wilderness. I was shoeless, cold, soaking wet and delirious. I was a shred of myself and mentally smashed to a pulp. While the paranoia that had been planted in my head with the purpose of disorienting and obstructing me from finding my dad had truly tested me to my core, it couldn't defeat me. Dom stayed with me, albeit virtually, until my connection was totally shut down, and then he came through for me in Peru.

I awoke with a grin and a sigh. I didn't need to recount my dreams from the night because this waking moment had all the tender truth I needed. I watched Dom stir awake. The second he opened his eyes they lit up at the sight of mine.

"I could get used to this," Dom said.

"You'd better."

Dom's peace and mine were just fine, but I had to keep my mom's in consideration as well. She knew I had some rekindling to do with my boyfriend, but I was well aware that she carried the burden of worry like no other. I had a responsibility to alleviate that concern. I had to get in touch with her since it was my first night staying back in my residence. It was high time to hop back on the grid. I wasn't prepared to reactivate my flex implant, so I took the old school route and pulled out my old clunky flexer, that, in its last position I had left it, was an earbud. When Dom hopped up to use the bathroom, I FigureFlexed my mom.

She deflected the FigureFlex and sent me a voice message.

*Hey, sweetie. I can't talk now—just let me know you're safe.*

I blinked at the message, taken aback. Where could she be this early in the morning that she couldn't talk?

*I am. Felt good to sleep in my own bed. Where are you?* I flexed her back.

*I'll flex you when you're out of session,* came her reply.

Oookay.

Her brief replies were unlike her, especially after everything we'd been through. If I knew my mom—and I do—she would have been asking me a bunch of questions to ensure I was healthy and safe, not rushing me off. Something was most definitely going on with her.

# 6

NO MATTER HOW much water I drank, the lump in my throat wouldn't budge. I kept trying because I'm no quitter. My feet were scorching as if I was walking on lava alas the gleaming, golden halls of S.E.R.C. were anything but molten. As I was about to walk into my quantum computing session after so many weeks away, my guts rumbled and the space between my eyeballs felt like a rubber band being pulled in both directions. The added unknowingness of my mom's odd behavior only compounded the stress of transitioning back into population with actual humans.

In Culver City, my math skills were wasted. At S.E.R.C., we were all top-tier scholars, but now I wasn't sure I cared anymore. Senecan scholars were the top echelon in every academic category. That's why they were recruited here—to help build an advanced society that would benefit and improve the world. Before I came to Seneca I wasn't proud of my math capabilities. I didn't try to do well on tests, and to be honest, I just didn't care. School was lame, and Mr. Malin's calculus class in L.A. sucked the life out of me. In contrast, from the moment I first arrived in S.E.R.C., I wanted to succeed. Up until recently I had been motivated to try hard so I could help bring about positive change in our world, but now I just wanted a simple, normal, teenage life.

I wondered what my session mates would think of my absence, or how far behind I had fallen academically in comparison to them. It didn't matter. This wasn't a competition. I was where I was whether or not I stressed out about it. I needed to quell the physical commotion I was experiencing rather than allowing my focus to be dominated by the unknowns around me.

I closed my eyes to let go of the outside and move inward. I rested my hands against my thighs and brought complete attention to this space—my temple. My hands tingled and warmed my muscles. I paid attention to my breath, and as that breath traveled down the column of my body, from my throat into my gut, the tension that permeated every inch of me began to dissolve. I breathed in deep, moving my focus further down my limbs into my feet where the heat always seemed to bubble up unbearably. I blew it all out my mouth and did it again. I traveled into the tips of my toes and recollected the frigid waters of the James River in Virginia where Dom and I had visited just after we first got our flex implants. Tapping into the memory of dipping our feet in that icy water cooled me down, and my heartbeat calmed.

Walking into the quantum computing room proved to be anti-climactic. Scholars were getting ready as the bell was set to ring. My session leader, Professor Brian Keatts, was advising Yoshi Higashi on a 3D interface as Yoshi manipulated it. It appeared to be controlling something on a screen that looked like a robot walking on grainy soil. The image was in infrared, so I couldn't totally make out the location or its exact terrain.

Yoshi Higashi was a unique kid I had seen on my first day in S.E.R.C. A robotics prodigy, he was apparently picked on so much growing up that he retreated into a shell of self-preservation, where he developed a robotic-self-defense system that could take on bullies—a system that included his own robotic arm, sleek and precise. Yoshi wasn't in my session last I recalled, but neither were half of the scholars in the room, and that was a surprise to me.

"Campbell, you're back," Professor Keatts announced in a dry tone as he looked up. This guy was lanky, and moved like a pasta noodle being dangled from someone's fingers. I'm pretty sure he wore the same gray outfit practically every single day, with only the slightest variation in geometric patterns on his crisp shirts. The scholars referred to him as "Professor Cookie" behind his back because it seemed like all he ever ate were oatmeal raisin cookies. I swear he was so mellow because they were laced.

"Yes, and ready to work," I replied.

"Okay then. Last month we brought in the bot lab for a cross-collaboration to create this fusion session: intergalactic bot programing. Your session mates have been paired up with the bot scholars. Yoshi here doesn't have a partner so you two are a team now. Go ahead and get acquainted."

Yoshi let out a grunt and wouldn't even look at me. It was bad enough that the bot lab kids thought they were more important than everyone else, but Yoshi had an extra chip on his shoulder that he carried all the way from childhood.

"Pep up, Yoshi," Professor Cookie, said, "Dorothy Campbell is—*was* the top quantum computing scholar in all of S.E.R.C. You should consider this collaboration an honor."

Ouch. The, "*was*," from Professor Cookie stung. Yoshi was expressionless, but at least that was better than cynical.

I extended my hand to Yoshi to formally introduce myself, "Doro."

He looked at my hand, then back to his screen.

"Oookay," I muttered to myself.

Professor Cookie moved on to another pair of scholars and left me with Yoshi, who apparently wasn't going to acknowledge that I was his partner. He continued to control the interface, which I noticed had a slight delay with the bot it was communicating with.

"Where are those bots?" I asked.

"Mars."

"What are they being used for?"

"These ones are experimental." His accent was thick. "They are not in the working bot population. We are testing command and response time programming."

Professor Keatts stood at the front of the room and cleared his throat.

"Scholars, in the past week of our collaboration you have successfully reduced the roundtrip transmission delay between the interface here in Seneca and the bots on Mars from six minutes thirty seconds to six twenty-nine, but I know that with your collective ingenuity, we can do better."

I leaned in to Yoshi, "I can make this zero."

Boom—Yoshi turned and looked at me with intrigued, yet skeptically raised eyebrows, like *are you serious?*

I whispered, "But I am not going to… unless I know what these bots are for."

"That is not the assignment."

"Is life all about taking assignments?"

Yoshi shrugged. I could tell he knew the answer but didn't want to throw me a bone.

I knew that, if I applied myself, I could bypass light-speed travel-delay by creating realtime two-way communication between a computer here in Seneca and the computing device in the bots on Mars with quantum entanglement. It would be just like the quantum entanglement of the nanobots S.O.I.L. had injected into the bloodstreams of Senecans. That particular entanglement, unbeknownst to the Senecan population, let brains communicate directly with the mainframe in Claytor Lake, and vice versa. This method was mind-blowing, next level in control from a distance. The thing is, theoretically distance should be a non-issue once two particles are entangled because it doesn't matter how far in the universe entangled particles are away from each other—once they are entangled, communication is instantaneous.

Despite the fact that I believed it could be done, I wasn't up to applying myself to the task. For starters, I knew it would be the most intricate coding challenge I'd ever taken on and that would contradict my new, "live simple," plan. On top of that, I was well aware that if I *did* take a stab at it, I would probably make it happen and, in turn, create the opportunity for the capabilities to fall into the wrong hands. I'd have to ensure that couldn't happen and I knew I couldn't be sure of that—yet. I also knew that with my old flexer I wouldn't be able to get past some of the coding road blocks, so I'd be required to reactivate my flex implant. As curious as I was about the whole thing, this was a rabbit hole I was not ready to step into, so for the rest of session I twiddled my thumbs and feigned involvement anytime Professor Keatts walked by. Yoshi and I didn't talk at all.

First and foremost, the only thing that was on my mind now that I knew my dad was alive, was that I had to find a way to reunite my family. I wasn't going to do anything that would jeopardize that, including anything to antagonize the Seneca Observation and Intelligence League. I felt like they were just chomping at the bit to bust me and Dom for anything.

I tried to flex my mom the second I walked out of session. Once again, she didn't answer. Mom never left me hanging like this. She was always the one checking in, making sure I was okay. Now it felt like she was slipping away. I suddenly felt a little woozy so I leaned back against the wall. My vision blurred, heat surged, and nausea hit me like a wave. I closed my eyes, attempting to imagine I was no longer here in S.E.R.C., and tried to recall that blissful, infinite expanse I had reached not so long ago… I wanted to go back there. My deep breaths brought my body temperature back down and the wooziness subsided.

# 7

AS MUCH AS I wanted to stay neutral and normal, an immense curiosity about those bots had crept into my thoughts. Who controlled the bots—Departers, FlexCorp, or someone else? What were their intentions? Did I really need to know, or was ignorance truly bliss? Ugh. Why was this so confusing and why the heck did I have to care?

Where was Reba? I'd flexed him yesterday—still nothing. Ellen said he was in the Aboves, but I couldn't shake my impatience. When would he return? No matter how hard I tried, I couldn't find that relaxed space. I had to keep moving forward. I checked my flexer again. Nothing. No messages from Reba. No word from my mom.

"Doro!" A girl's enthused voice from a ways away brought my inner-questionnaire to a halt. I peered down the golden hall to see Brittany Gilroy and G.W. Wallingsford eagerly headed in my direction.

"Brittany!" I was excited to see her, and even G.W., too.

"Hey, Doro from L.A.," G.W., said as I hugged them both.

"What's up, G.W.?"

It appeared by their hand-holding that they were currently in the "on" position of their on-again-off-again relationship.

"Where you been?" G.W., asked.

"Long story," I replied.

"I'd love to hear it, but I'm on a tight schedule today. You two have fun playing catch up."

"Bye, babe," Brittany purred and kissed G.W., like they were a new couple, but in actuality they'd been dating, much to their parents' influence, for several years.

G.W. sauntered off, greeting other scholars along the way like the good son of a politician. G.W. was undeniably the man in S.E.R.C., and even though he was a Wallingsford and fitted the typical All-American jock profile to a T, I kind of liked the guy.

"Want to skip lunch and go for a ride?" Brittany asked.

"You read my mind."

Brittany, like G.W., was the daughter of a Seneca Senator. Only her dad, Senator Gilroy, was a Repairer, whereas G.W.'s dad, Senator Frank Wallingsford, was a Departer. I wondered if they both knew of their parents' respective allegiances. Part of me wanted to go fishing to find out, but I nipped that line of thought in the bud for a focus on fun.

The incredible equine facility where the Gilroy family kept their horses was a breath of fresh air, literally and figuratively. The sprawling, verdant-green pasture, with its blades of grass that tickled my ankles made me feel as if we were in a real Virginia meadow. Somehow, there was a gentle breeze that came and went, sending tide-like waves through the sea of green. I took a gigantic breath of the pungent earthiness. Smells like these were a major scarcity these days. The scent of grass sat so heavy in the back of my throat I could taste it. With my nose high to the wind, I savored the flavor of the earth I had met in Virginia and released a happy sigh. L.A. was a sun-dried concrete jungle that never gave me this. Neither would Mars, I imagined… and the possibility that I could explore that was growing.

Brittany and I led the horses out from the stables. I was with Athena the Paint again, and she was with her Palomino, Prince. He was named after the singer that died long before we were born. Brittany loved the song 'Purple Rain,' and our shared interest in music was one of the things we connected on. As we made our way out into the pasture, Brittany gracefully hopped up on Prince. With more confidence than I'd had in the recent past, I did the same. I'd only had my first ride on a horse less than a year ago, when I was on the run from S.O.I.L. with Dom in

Southwestern Virginia.

"It feels so good to be back out here again," I said to Brittany.

"Right? This never gets old."

"You think Athena remembers me?"

"Yes! She for sure knows you."

Athena nickered at me and that brought a smile to my face. "Hey, girl," I said as I stroked her neck near her wiry, pepper-colored mane.

Brittany slowed her horse so that we rode side-by-side. "So," she said, "I've heard the rumors, and I don't want to pry, but—"

"It's okay. Most of it is probably true," I said.

Brittany sighed, "Sorry that happened to you, Doro. Are you okay now?"

I nodded, but shrugged. "I think so, but who knows? There is too much going on around us to know for sure, right? And maybe I would be better off not knowing about any of it."

"That's why I love it *here*."

"I get it. Believe me, I'd rather be here riding Athena and Prince with you than out there in the madness."

Brittany nodded. "It's just so crazy—all of it. It's like, I hear my parents talking politics, and I know enough to know it's complicated and I don't want to know any more."

She did know something, though, and now since she had

brought it up, I could be blunt. “So, you *do* know about Mars and the whole Departer-Repairer conflict?”

Brittany took a beat. “What I do know is that my dad is so consumed by all of that, that it feels like my family lost him to it, and this conflict is here to stay. I hate it.”

“Ahh. I get that.”

“I know you do, Doro, and I know that’s why you went on your mission to South America. To try and bring your family back together.”

I nodded, “And now, after all that I went through, I wanted so badly to believe what will happen, will happen and I can’t change that.”

Even as I said that to Brittany, and even though this moment with her felt like a great relief, my inner-voice was yelling at me, *‘Your calling is not to conform! You CAN change things!’*

“Hmm,” Brittany squinted in thought, “I have to say I am really intrigued with what happened down there, but what I’ve really been dying to know, after all this time—did you find him?”

I smiled.

“I knew it!” Brittany exclaimed, her eyes glowing. “Oh, Doro, I am so happy for you!”

The horses’ hooves sunk into the mossy trail, and I leaned forward to stroke my mare’s neck. The calm rhythm of her gait settled something restless in me. For the first time in what felt like weeks, I could breathe.

But then—a glint caught my eye. A flash of silver on the stalk of a tree. I slowed my horse, squinting. Embedded in the bark, half-hidden by a tangle of ivy, was a tiny SurveilSpike. The device's lens pulsed faintly, like it was alive.

My stomach tightened. Someone was watching. Even here, in this pocket of untouched tranquility.

I swallowed hard, my voice dropping to a whisper. "I hope the story has a happy ending," I said to Brittany, "but I just don't know what's going to happen yet."

She glanced at me, her smile softening. "It will all work out. You'll see." she said, "I think we just have to put our trust in our dads and know they aren't making selfish decisions. The only other thing I can do is pray."

I hoped she was right. I needed a break from questioning people's motives, and in this moment that wasn't happening. I was feeling grateful. "Brittany, thank you for bringing me here. I needed this more than I even knew."

"Oh, I am so happy to have someone to hang out with who loves this as much as I do."

I brought myself back to the flow of the horseback ride. Listening to hooves thump. Smelling the pungency of the grass. Being with a friend who understood me. This peaceful place and these sweet creatures brought me so much joy, but there was still the slightest hint of unease streaming through my veins because the horse was ten times my size and she had all the control over what she would do next, regardless of what I instructed her to do. I kept facing this vulnerability: trusting something—or someone—beyond myself. Athena and I shared a quiet bond, but there was no telling what she'd do next. Still, I couldn't let the unknown ruin the joy of the moment. I could request her to stop by pulling back on the reins, but she might resist and go faster. Or something from another direction might spook her and cause her to kick and me to fall. There was just no telling what could happen, yet I felt the unknown future shouldn't be able to kill the joy of the moment, or my connection with Athena. It seemed that the very nature of life was that we could never be certain of what anyone else would do and part of my journey was how I accepted that.

As I followed Brittany and Prince into a trot, the rhythm felt good and it sunk in deeper that things will forever arise unexpectedly. I couldn't predict the future, but I could trust the flow—and maybe, that was enough.

# 8

I TOSSED TO my left and then my right. Feeling hot and clammy, I threw my covers off, then got the chills and bundled myself back under them. I repeated this over and over again, unable to regulate my temperature. My bed was an ice box and a sauna, my mind a race flighter with no brakes. I was happy to be back in my own bed in my residence but I was also annoyed with myself that I couldn't just sleep like a normal human being. Instead of letting this restlessness amp up, I sat up in bed and activated my flexer. I saw I had a missed flex from my mom, the message floating in the air before me, translucent and glowing. Finally!

*Hey, sweetie, I wanted to say goodnight and let you know I've been pulled into some overtime shifts helping at the clinic in my residence. There is nothing to worry about. Talk soon. xx*

It was too late to flex her back. I didn't want her to be

alarmed by a message from me in the middle of the night.

I flipped B3 on.

Video images played: dozens of robots and rovers moving about over volcanic black rocks, collecting geological samples and showing readings on screens as nearby scientists took it all in.

A woman's voice spoke over the images: *"Current stages in robotic testing show how these rovers navigate the rough terrain and tectonic fissures around the Great Basalt Wall in Australia."*

I watched a video of a complete habitat set up: a city constructed of marshmallow colored domes with satellites on top, with each unit connected by clear, above-ground tunnels.

*"Senecans in Hub 84 are going through rigorous training for Mars departures. They are acclimatizing to conditions that mimic those which will be experienced on the Martian planet. Here, they are learning how to adapt and live on the inhospitable new terrain."*

Pipe was being laid, bricks molded, built, and placed in super-speed production lines. Entire buildings were being erected at mind-boggling velocity. Structures I'd seen take months to build in Los Angeles were on course to be done in a day on Mars. I knew there was way more to what was going on with Seneca's settlement of Mars than meets the eye. There always was when it came to this secret society. I thought about my resistance to the challenge in the bot lab session. I knew it stemmed from a fear of my findings falling into the wrong hands. I had no idea what the bots were doing, what they were capable of, or who was controlling them. But what if I *did* know? What if I could secretly discover how to communicate with them across the galaxy in real-time?

If I could harness a quantum entanglement communication system, I might bypass the constraints of traditional data transmission—creating instantaneous links across vast distances—literally, instant messages across galaxies. If *I* tapped into their programing, how much more would I know about what was going on?

God knows my dad probably had no idea what they were doing considering he was so far entrenched in Doromium studies underground, on a completely different part of the planet. I imagined I could be an extension of my my dad and find out for him the information he didn't have access to. We could be a dream team again. My dad had made all of these advances possible after all, with his discovery of an element that could not only repair our atmosphere on Earth but also build one on another planet, far off in the solar system. It was up to me to protect his legacy.

I could not deny the intriguing nature of the stuff that wasn't spoon fed to me by way of B3 Media or what I was told in session. Did I dare break the rules again to uncover the truth?

The question was irrelevant—I knew I would. It was like those shady bots were laid out in front of me like an apple in the Garden of Eden—juicy and ripe for a big ol' bite.

No wonder I couldn't sleep. How could my brain possibly shut down when there was still so much to know? I had danced with death, but I was not dead and therein was the case in point—I was here for a reason and the universe was sending me this messaging: Close the time delay. Why? B3 will show you. Oh, what's that you say, dear universe? There is more to uncover? Dive in, Doro! My heart jolted, I grabbed at my chest and gasped. Was I experiencing ghost palpitations? I turned off my flexer and laid back in the dark. I couldn't shut down the speed of my spinning mind, but I didn't want to. My gut said let it run, your mind is your gift. Use it well.

I could not rest knowing that, as I sat there twiddling my thumbs in the dark, other S.E.R.C. scholars would climb to the top of the mountain of information and hand it all over to elitist monsters who definitely wouldn't handle it with positive intent.

Even though it was the middle of the night, I had to try to get in touch with Reba again. He was the one friend who would dive deep with me to a level most people were incapable of. I longed for Reba's honesty. It was possible that he hadn't received my flexes, so I flexed him again. It was one of a half-dozen flexes I'd popped off so far, to which there were no replies. It didn't add up. He was always there—unless something, or someone, was keeping him away. The thought chilled me more than the night air. I hoped he would be in touch in the morning. In the meantime, I told myself, I needed to get some rest so I could tackle those communication lines to the bots on Mars, and close the time delay. If I could do that, I would be at the helm of interplanetary—no, *interstellar* communication.

# 9

In my perpetual waking state of agitation, the universe, by way of B3, reminded me of the strides being made with the bot testing near the Great Basalt Wall. The picture painted by B3 was aggressively progressive, but I knew that sword was double-edged. My curiosity bubbled to a boil. Even though being with my mom, my boyfriend, my dog, my friends, and the sweet horses was pretty darn blissful, I reminded myself that I couldn't kill time just chillin' or time might kill us all. On top of that, I was growing more and more concerned with the safety of my mom and Reba. Why were they so M.I.A.? It was easy to let my mind spin off in its own elaborate storytelling, but I had to reel it in in the spirit of productivity.

The dark silence of night vanished without a trace, pushing me forward into session whether I was ready or not. This time I wasn't nervous, though. I traipsed in with a self-assurance so fresh I practically bounced like I was on springs. I did realize I needed to get a robotics scholar like Yoshi on my side, and this would be no easy task. I was a math girl, not a lobbyist. Since Yoshi was a robotics junkie, my approach would be to paint him a picture of what we could do if we worked together, in extreme and utter confidentiality, of course. We could achieve a kind of exclusive techno access he'd never experienced before. If I wanted this guy to pay me the least bit of attention, I had to speak his language.

I took a seat at the desk next to Yoshi. Enthralled in a graphic novel as he waited for session to begin, he didn't even acknowledge me. He used his finger in the air to flip the virtual pages. I sized him up before leaning in to whisper, "What if I told you, I could make one of those Martian bots yours?"

Yoshi squinted ever so slightly and squeezed his lips as if he'd just tasted a lemon, but he didn't lift his gaze from the graphics. He scrolled through, seemingly oblivious to my presence, but I knew better.

"Never mind," I said. "Maybe you're not interested in having your very own bot to explore the martian planet, without anyone knowing."

I could see his interest was piqued. He was obviously pretending to look at his graphic novel, but I knew my suggestion was too enticing to resist. I continued, "Imagine being the first scholar to ever have that kind of access. Just you and the bot. But it doesn't sound like you're into it, so never mind."

He looked away from his flex screen and quipped, "I thought you did not want to participate in the assignment."

"Yeah. I didn't change my mind about that."

Yoshi shook his head and picked his screen back up.

"But that isn't what I asked you," I clarified.

"If you do not do the assignment, how will you get me one of the bots?" He asked.

I knew I could break the time delay, but I also knew I needed Yoshi's help in order to fully understand the coding and controls on the bots. I would absolutely have to complete this line of discovery or else my work could be swiped up and weaponized.

I spoke in a super-hushed tone. "Okay, look, I *do* want to try my hand at closing the time delay, but I *don't* want to hand any work over to Professor Cookie—Keatts… yet."

"Why not?"

"Because I want to see what the bots are for and why they want us to do this assignment to begin with."

"I see." The wheels were turning just behind his shrinking and expanding pupils. Yoshi Higashi was catching my gist.

"If we help each other on this we can both have what we want," I added.

"As long as I am not breaking any rules, I might agree."

I knew that *I* would be breaking some sort of rules, but *Yoshi* wouldn't. He just needed to translate what was on the screen for me. So technically, this was a deal we could make. I nodded, "Okay, so… partners?"

Yoshi lifted up his robotic arm and stuck his machine hand out to shake mine made of flesh. It felt ironic that I was shaking hands with a robot. Without another word, we turned to the screen in front of us and I immediately thrust myself into the zone, writing code to take a stab at closing the time-delay. It was just basic stuff. I wrapped my code in quantum encryption—if anyone tried to intercept it, the message would self-destruct. Six minutes twenty-nine seconds after I sent my first command to the Martian bot we had been assigned to, I got a message back. Yoshi could tell by my crinkled nose and squinty eyes that I wasn't adept at translating bot feedback. He offered up an explanation, "The bot is granting limited access."

Hmm. I sat back. Limited access wasn't going to cut it. Complete access was the objective, but I was well aware it wasn't going to come that easy. If I had any inclination about who was behind the defense systems there, I would have known what level of application I needed to work my way around them. I sent a message back to retrieve the full parameters of the programming matrix within which I could work. Six minutes, twenty-nine seconds later I was in the matrix. This delay was horrific! Now that I had this, I *could* start the assignment and work on closing the delay between the command given here in my session and when it was received on Mars. Instead, I wanted to dig into the outskirts of this access area that was disclosed to us.

Yoshi sat up straight and on the edge of his seat. "Looks like we have a five foot radius to make it roll."

"We'll get to that," I said, "I just want to see a little bit more about what this guy can do."

"Okay." Yoshi watched intently as I punched in code to break through the permissions granted to the bot lab. "What are you doing now?" He asked.

"Hang tight. You'll get your bot. Just let me see…" My voice trailed off as my fingers danced across the keys. It had been a while since I'd been in my happy place and it felt electric. My body buzzed with fiery focus, feet planted, mind dancing with the code. I told myself, "Doro, breathe."

A section of programming within the bots that had not been disclosed in the programming matrix unexpectedly opened up.

Yoshi looked back and forth between me and the screen.

"What is that?" he asked.

I couldn't admit to Yoshi that I had found complete access to this section of the programming. I didn't trust him enough to make him privy to the extent of my digging, only the bits and pieces that were crucial for him to know in order for us to push forward. I intended to keep my end of the bargain and give him what I promised—realtime access to a martian bot, but I couldn't read this bot communication matrix and I needed to know what it meant.

"Can you read this?" I asked.

"Yes. It's basically a 'kill' command."

I was taken aback, "Kill what? What kind of kill?"

"I can't tell. It's tied to a program that has not been installed."

I could see the reference to a program, but there was no clear source of where it was coming from. My eyes widened as my heartbeat escalated and breaths became shallow. Adrenaline surged—sharp, exhilarating. The code mirrored what I'd uncovered at Claytor Lake with Ellen, an echo of the same elusive truth. Back then, I had sent a coding through the channel that was coming in and out of my flex implant and it mirrored back to me, just like this one. I recalled how I had to beat the offense at its own game to reveal that Flex Technology Corporation was the source of the bug. I tried my hand at the same tactic here by applying the same coding, but I didn't get the same outcome. I was hitting a brick wall. It was going to take more to bust through it.

Yoshi was suddenly peering at a line of messaging coming from the bots back to us. "That is crazy," he exclaimed.

"What?" I scooted myself to the edge of my seat and

turned to Yoshi.

“Hmm.” He scratched his chin with his robotic finger.

“Tell me!” I peered at him and then spun my eyes back to the screen so that we both sat with our faces inches from the code.

Yoshi spoke with his eyes glued to the screen. “This kill program can be initiated by someone who could be anywhere in the universe if they are connected to the bots… and if this is right, it also says there are 248,832 output locations in the program’s scope… and on top of that…” Yoshi took a step back from the console, he pointed to subtle markers in the bot coding. “See this? It was deliberately designed to lure analysts into a trap. I have seen it before. It implies there is an entity anticipating resistance.” His voice dropped into a tight whisper. “Whoever put this here... they knew someone would find it eventually.” He turned to me, his jaw clenched.

I replied, “So, someone inside this program knew we would seek, and they want us to fail?” I asked this question more to myself than to him. “How can we even begin to make sense of that?”

“I don’t have an answer or a theory. The program overrides the computing systems—also unlike any bot communication system I have ever seen.” He was totally baffled and totally into it. We were on to something. There was no turning back.

I agreed, "I know computing systems like the back of my hand. But it doesn't look like anything I have ever seen, either, and the bot language is completely foreign to me. We need to find out where the people are that are connected to it, and what exactly the kill switch is."

"I can not do that. I can just tell you what the bot's response is when we issue a command to it."

"That's all I need from you," I assured him. "Right now I'm going to build a simple line of spy-coding which will infect every bot on Mars that is in network with this bot. Then, when someone accesses the kill program, for any reason, it will send a message to our Veils and we will be alerted in flex so we can see where the program has been accessed from."

Professor Keatts appeared behind us, "Campbell, Higashi."

I jumped, but played it off as Yoshi let out a nervous, "Yes, sir."

"Looks like you two are getting along quite well."

Yoshi sat back and gulped. He wouldn't look at Professor Keatts. I compensated for Yoshi's guilty demeanor. "Yoshi isn't too sure that we can do this, but I am, Professor Keatts."

"Good to see you back at work, Miss Campbell."

"It's good to be back." I meant it. If there was a curtain in front of us, I was the girl to yank it back, even though Gregory

Zaffron and others had warned me about what would happen if I even so much as tried. I spent the rest of session bouncing questions and answers back and forth with Yoshi. He told me what the bots' messages said and I wrote our coding. I couldn't close the time delay, but that was okay. For now I just wanted to be connected to this Martian robotic network so I could determine who was pulling the strings and what exactly those strings were. I believed the way to achieve this would be by installing a malware on the Martian bot which was assigned to Yoshi and me. Theoretically, this would give me access to the whole network, even those outside of the test group we were working with. Now there was an even bigger question: why was this program outputting to almost a quarter million locations?

# *10*

DOM AND I flexed that we would meet up to grab something to eat and say goodnight. I didn't even hint that I had anything important to talk about—I knew better than that. We kept real talk face-to-face. The grid was too risky. S.O.I.L. was no dumb-dumb agency. It annoyed me to be back in the incognito frame of mind I had ditched. It just wasn't conducive to the joyful state I had tasted when I was down for the count. In theory, living as a normal teenager sounded super chill, but in reality, I knew deep down I wouldn't be satisfied as a complacent girl in a rapidly evolving world. As the complexities of the systems in which we were enmeshed became exposed, so amped up my elemental drive to seek and stand up for the truth.

Dom was just as set as I was to relax and assume the role of an actual teenager instead of an enemy of the state. He, like me, had been consumed with uncovering, running, hiding and fighting, and even though we'd made great strides, we got beat down. After sitting alongside my comatose body for fifty-four days, Dom was just plain fatigued. The guy had lost his spirit, and I missed it. But I understood.

I had requested we skip Ty's Sushi in favor of the loudest place in the Restaurant District: The Cantina. Even though I preferred Dia De Los Ninos, this place could satisfy my chilaquiles fix and it would be loud enough to diffuse our discussion. The moment a basket of warm corn chips hits the table always jolted my spirits. I couldn't enjoy the food fully this time though, because my focus fell on reconnecting with a subdued Dom.

Dom's trademark piercing look had softened, his biggest concern now being how much heat the salsa packed. He wasn't into kicks and spices like I was. I attributed that to his East Coast Italian upbringing and all that mild pasta and mozzarella, but this demeanor wasn't about something so trivial as an aversion to jalapeños.

"You okay?" I asked.

"Yeah," He said, unconvincingly.

"You're so quiet."

"Just tired."

"Me too." I actually wasn't, but it just slipped out because I wanted him to feel heard. After a moment of sitting there, I just couldn't resist.

"I found out some stuff today."

"I had a feeling," he replied.

"Did you?"

Dom sat back and nodded. "I knew it was only a matter of time."

"Yeah, well. It's crazy, Dom."

Dom leaned in close to me. "Okay. Give it to me."

I turned my mouth right next to his ear and whispered. "There are bots on Mars. Thousands of them. And they aren't just there for testing soil and setting up habitats."

"Not surprising."

"There's some creepy kill switch in their programming."

"Shocker." He was totally unfazed.

"I know, but just because we're getting used to this sort of thing doesn't mean we should ignore it, right?"

"Depends. What do you think they're planning on doing?" he asked, hesitantly, as if he didn't even want to know.

"It's more like, what *aren't* they planning on doing? You know what they're capable of."

Dom bit the inside of his lip and dropped into thought, but he quickly shook that off and looked pleadingly at me. It is crazy how much more his eyes ever spoke to me than his words. "I get it, Doro, but I don't want to think about that stuff right now. Can't we just be here, together?"

"We are. I'm here." I said, and then forced myself to stop speaking for a second.

"But?"

"But how can we turn a blind eye to what's right in front of us?"

"That's exactly what I'm saying." Dom sat back and spread his arms open like 'look at me'.

I totally got it. He just wanted us to be here in the simpleness of the moment, untouched by the chaos. Butterflies fluttered up to my chest and in a flash my heart told me to relax. My shoulders dropped and I sat back. This was amazing and all, but there were strong tugs inching in. Getting lost in the moment with Dom felt amazing and his sweet romantic sentiment really got me good, but this wasn't sustainable.

"So, what do you want to talk about, the weather?"

His eyes narrowed and then he relaxed and sat back. "Okay. You know what? If something is on your mind, then it's on mine, too."

There weren't many people I knew, if any, that heard me the way he did. I pushed myself up and leaned across the table to kiss him. His lips made my head spin. My eyes stayed shut and eyebrows lifted, chilaquiles and bots off my mind.

"Okay then, let's talk bots if that's how it makes you feel," Dom said with a grin.

"Easy. Bots are hardly a turn on," I said with a little laugh. "They're actually super creepy."

Dom nodded. "Of course there's noway they're only

working to build infrastructure."

"So, what, are they being established as extensions of S.O.I.L., like prison guards?"

"Who knows. I wouldn't put *anything* past them."

"Exactly, so instead of overthinking it and becoming paranoid, I want to figure it out," I said.

"You can't let this put you back in a bad place, Doro."

"It won't. I'll keep a clear head, which shouldn't be hard considering my implant's deactivated."

The second I said that, I felt dishonest because my gut said reactivation was imminent.

Dom nodded half-heartedly. He was obviously still unsure about meddling.

"The citizens, the scholars, none of us have full access to everything the bots are doing," I told him.

"Even if we did know exactly what was up, what do you really think we could do about it?"

"You're taking this pretty lightly, Dom. It's like you don't have faith in us."

"*Us* is what I want to protect. I can't go through losing you again."

The gravity of Dom's experience sunk in. I did want O.G. Dom back—the guy with fire in his eyes and a focus so hot he leaves a blaze on his trail, but at the same time I watched him struggle to hold onto the idea of a peaceful life. The memory of those fifty-four days—sitting next to my motionless body—was etched into his eyes. I got it. I really did. But we couldn't let that fear keep us from the truth.

"Remember when you came to me about the nanobots in the blood of Seneca Citizens?" I asked him. "Just think—what if I hadn't been curious, too? Imagine if we hadn't joined forces to attack that head on. Imagine where we would all be right now."

"I get it, Doro," he said with his voice fading and his eyes closed. But I also sensed that undying spark inside him. I just needed to fan the flame.

"Dom. There is an entire network set up on a planet in outer space, where *we* are set to go."

"*We*?"

"You know what I mean—*Senecans*. The bots there can do everything we can. Their wiring literally mimics that in our own brains, the programming is just like the neuro-data we discovered in Claytor Lake, but I don't know exactly where it's coming from. It's not just that either, it contains coding extremely similar to what I found on my flex implant hack, but I don't get the same results when I play with the code. These things aren't just computers doing predictable sequences, this is next-level."

When he clenched his jaw and leaned in, the spark blazed back to life. There he was—my Dom.

"Okay," he said, "but we have to do things differently

this time."

"Agreed." I kept my cool.

"We need to align with people that have a real deep knowledge of the system and also have pull inside Seneca."

"We have Ellen," I said.

"Ellen is questionable."

"Everyone is questionable," I retorted.

"True," he said.

"But she's tenacious, intelligent and she's proven her loyalty to me *and* my dad."

"Okay. We need someone else. Someone with a knowledge of Seneca, of the system, who really, actually cares more about justice than appeasing power players."

We both fell silent as we thought: Who, who, who? And then it hit me. "I got it. My Seneca Civics & Ethics session leader, Richmond Shields. The guy is some kind of spiritual guru *and* an expert on the system. That's why he was chosen to teach us."

Dom rubbed his chin and bit the inside of his cheek. I could see the wheels turning and I loved it.

"But he's a leader in S.E.R.C., he's tied directly to the authorities."

"Everyone is tied directly to the authorities. You could say the same thing about you and me, recruited straight up by Ellen Malone and the men in black knocking at our doors. Or in your case, juvie." I smiled.

"Okay, okay," he said. "I see your point. But we need to be very careful, Doro."

"Are you really telling *me* to be careful?"

Dom smiled, "I know we can't just let this stuff go, but I so want *this* to last. You and me. I want this so bad. No bots, no S.O.I.L., no hacked flex implants. Just us. Sitting together, happily eating terrible Mexican food—"

"*Terrible*!? Are you crazy?! This is heaven on Earth!"

"*In* Earth, you mean."

For as serious a guy as Dom was, he could always make me laugh.

"I love you, Doro. I'm all-in to figure this out with you, but we can't let the insanity tear us away from what matters most."

"We won't."

Dom got up, walked over to my side of the booth and slid in next to me. I wanted to freeze this moment—just us, a distant island untouched by the madness crashing around us. But love wasn't about staying safe. It was about stepping into the fire, together. They say be careful what you ask for, and I say screw that. When Dom looked at me, his eyes burned with the sort of intensity that dared the universe to push back. This was the Dom I fell for. The Dom who faced chaos head-on and made me believe we could survive it. He ran his hand through my hair on the back of my head and pulled me in for a kiss. The kiss wasn't gentle; it was a storm breaking after a long drought, raw and fierce.

# *11*

WE WERE BACK on the clock after I shockingly had a full night of good rest and my alarm jolted me awake. Just after seven in the morning, Dom and I sat face-to-face with Richmond Shields and Ellen Malone, downloading them on the sketchy, secret robot situation with their unsettling kill command. Ellen had brought us to a place that is a dead zone within S.E.R.C. for S.O.I.L. tracing—a cavern of calcite crystal formations surrounded by lead. It was similar to where they held the Senate hearings, but just a fraction of the size. This was a space they preserved for S.E.R.C. scholars to come for meditation; a space that I should probably use more, but today, on my first visit to the cavern, I was far from meditating. My mouth moved a mile a minute, trying to keep up with the information that cascaded out of my brain. As the words surged from me I could see Ellen and Professor Shields trying to keep up and process it all. It was a lot.

The night before, I had let Ellen know I was pulling Professor Shields into our inner circle. She didn't object to that in spite of his lack of clearance. Ellen was an incredible listener and I think that's why she retained so much information. Her typical, stoic gaze was unwavering as she processed and responded to what I was saying with poise. She seemed unaffected by my words and the more I unloaded, the more I wondered why she had no reaction. Literally zero. Meanwhile, Professor Shields, had an onslaught of questions. Full-disclosure on our part was crucial to bringing him up to speed, so Dom and I ran through every detail of the deceptions in the society that we had experienced.

We started with the Necrolla Carne vaccinations that S.O.I.L. required for every citizen of Seneca, which were actually nanobots injected into people's blood to trace our actions and behaviors. Professor Shields wanted to understand the ins and outs of the nanobots, how we discovered them, and who exactly came after us. We explained it all, and moved along to when Flex Technology Corporation bugged my flex implant to use me as a pawn in the game. We explained the purpose of my dad's discovery of Doromium to heal the planet's ozone layer, and the Departers weaponizing it. I told him how my dad had gone missing, and then as my life unfolded inside Seneca I found my DNA match in the Senecan database. I went on a trek to locate that individual in a South American hub—I just knew it would be my dad, and it was. My whole story landed just a few days back with Yoshi and I finding the elusive kill switch command in the Martian robots. Professor Shields nodded and listened intently. When I finished speaking, my words hung in the air like static. Shields's eyes narrowed as he absorbed each piece of the puzzle. A bead of sweat traced down his temple—I knew something was boiling inside him.

Finally, Ellen spoke up. "That was quite the summation, you guys. First off, I want you to know, we are on your side—"

Dom expelled a little 'yeah right' grunt to interrupt Ellen. Ellen didn't let that fly, "Dom, I understand that you've had your reservations about me since day one, but if you expect us to move forward on the same page, you're going to have to let that go."

I was intimately aware of Dom's wariness of Ellen, and I really didn't want it to put a hiccup in our momentum. It was crucial that we joined forces. I shot laser beams at him from my eyes, but he was locked on Ellen, and she right back on him. Dom sat forward towards her, "Great sentiment, but you haven't exactly been on our side before."

"I am here now, aren't I?"

Dom shrugged that off. "Then why haven't *you* investigated the bots if you knew about them? Why did it take *us* to tell *you* that there is a kill switch?"

"There are plenty of things I know that you don't, and

vice versa. That is just the nature of perspective. Knowing everything and working tirelessly for the greater good are two completely different things."

I had to say, "Ellen is right, Dom."

"But so are we," he quipped back.

I felt he was being unreasonable towards Ellen and even though I had his back, I had to speak up for what was right, "And that is why we are all here, so we can combine everything we all know into one mega data set."

"Exactly," Ellen affirmed, "and even then there will *still* be more to know."

"Couldn't have said it better myself," Richmond said.

"Fair enough." Dom said.

Then it hit me. This, too, could be the nature of the bots. Compiling one collective set of intelligence from all of Seneca's data in order to form one mega-intelligence-cloud.

All three of them turned to me, and for the first time, in literally my entire life, I felt I had the support of one hundred percent of the room. Dom, Ellen and Professor Shields all believed in me. It wasn't because I was clamoring for their approval, it was because I had total faith in myself and our ability to change the trajectory of Seneca for the greater good. I inhaled a power breath through my nose, puffing up my chest and tilting my forehead back to invite that potent universal force that was far superior to a mojo stick. Without thinking about what I needed to say, my gut shoved the words right out of my mouth, “We need to dedicate ourselves to working together, to being honest with each other, to fighting through whatever obstacles are thrown at us, and to bring an end to the injustices once and for all. Not everyone is aware of the level of control that might overtake us, but we are. We can’t let the future be a prison of invisible walls and robotic guards. If we don’t act now, freedom becomes a memory. Everyone should know everything. Full transparency, period.”

“Absolutely!” Dom asserted.

Ellen nodded, “One hundred percent, Doro.”

Professor Shields quietly opined from a different angle, “It’s admirable that you two want to make a difference.”

I sensed in his apprehensively mild tone that he wasn’t coming out guns-a-blazing with us. He continued, “Full transparency? That’s a pipe dream in a state run society, but let’s look at what is most important here. What is your end goal?”

“Truth and freedom. People not being manipulated or controlled,” I quipped.

“Right.” Shields nodded, “So let’s look at how to take action on your objective.”

He had my ears, and Ellen’s, and Dom’s, too.

“Just think—the very reason B3 is feeding the masses the allure of migrating to Mars is because someone wants it to be fed to us. And why?”

"To get people amped up about departing," I answered, "and I think the idea of living in space is insanely cool, too—on the surface. But it's not all about the surface."

Shields nodded. "Right. This is simply history repeating itself on a much flashier scale. What we're looking at is no different than Christopher Columbus being funded by Spain, or Captain Cook bankrolled by the British, or Ferdinand Magellan—these guys were all backed by the kings and queens looking for new ways to add to their wealth. Think about Russia staking their flag at the bottom of the Arctic Ocean, which has been under ice for as long as humans have been exploring. They did that in anticipation of the ice caps melting and one day becoming Russian land. This is the next level of the same behavior. Seneca has become like its own country trying to lay claim to Mars—

"If Departers have their way, everyone will have to go and be under their rule," Dom added.

Shields nodded again. "Absolute power on an interplanetary level."

Ellen agreed. "Richmond is correct. Doro and Dominic, you two have tasted the measures they will go to to make sure it happens."

"It's crazier than what happened in the past though," I added. "Imagine having your mind and body policed twenty-four-seven by an army of robots that no country could ever build a counterforce against."

Shields swiftly interjected, "I don't disagree with you guys. At this point, anything is possible. It will all be quite alluring, though. Just picture it. Early Senecan settlers will be given all sorts of benefits before massive human habitation. It's already being set up this way. Just as it was for the first Brits who came to America. You take the risk, you get the reward."

"Then how do we let people know what's going on before it is too late?" I asked, and looked to Professor Shields.

"So, this is what I would ask. If what you're suggesting is in fact happening—one: how, without getting caught, do you determine exactly *who* is, and *how* they are creating that robotic, policed state, and then two: have you thought about a way to relay this information to the public?"

I sucked in a huge breath, held it at the top and waited for the answer to come to me, but it didn't. My balloon deflated. Dom and I looked at each other, hoping the other would have the answer. Nope.

Professor Shields nodded, "Okay then. We all know there are various factions and groups inside Seneca, and the only way to succeed in uniting people to overcome the oppression of any one of those groups, is to give the power to the people. This is about fighting for free will. You need to create a movement. Nothing ever happened without someone creating a movement."

Shields was right. In order to give the power back to the people, we needed the knowledge to be free and available to all, and there was one medium in place that would allow such a massive distribution of information inside Seneca: "B3," I said.

Ellen turned to Professor Shields, "Julian Hollenbeck."

Shields nodded with a smile, "Great guy, I know him well."

I had a lightbulb go off, too. "I remember learning that he came to Seneca because he was offered the chance to be cured of an 'untreatable' cancer. He was given a second shot at life here."

"This is true," Shields said, "and I can assure you, he is not unlike the Intuerians in this way, of wanting another shot at life and deeply appreciating the fact that Seneca provided it."

Dom nodded. "That's why I agreed to join S.E.R.C.'s molecular biology program. For a second chance."

I took Dom's hand and said, "Seneca isn't the problem. Seneca is what brought us together."

Ellen, having been at the forefront of Seneca's recruitment, reminded us, "There are a lot of people that were given a chance for something pretty spectacular here in Seneca, and that is what we are fighting for."

We all agreed on that. The Intuerians were treated as sub-human outcasts in the Aboves, and given an opportunity to grow and succeed in Seneca. I realized that, above all else, Reba's allegiance was to the Intuerians because he sympathizes and appreciates the honor Seneca provides them. The Intuerians in Seneca may or may not subscribe to the specific agendas and methods of the Departers, but they see the powers-that-be in that faction as having afforded them an opportunity to live, and live well. We couldn't blame them for taking sides based on that sentiment alone. Regardless, that didn't mean I was going to let Departer corruption spread like wildfire at the expense of everyone else's freedom.

At this point, I knew the steps that needed to occur. "Let's go get our confirmation, proof, and any information we can gather and go to Hollenbeck with a full deck."

The truth felt like a grenade with the pin pulled—dangerous, inevitable, waiting to explode.

As I left the room that morning, Ellen hurried after me and tapped my shoulder. "Doro, there's something I have wanted to speak with you about."

Uh-oh. "Okay."

Ellen's stoic mask cracked for just a second, her eyes clouded with something unspoken.

"I've had something on my mind for quite a while and in the spirit of truth, I have to admit something."

"Sure." I sensed a shame she was holding on to. It was hidden there behind her sunken eyes and I could tell this was a vulnerability that the one and only Ellen Malone was unaccustomed to. She suddenly felt more human than the enigma I'd once seen her as.

"When you first came to Seneca and we took our flighter trip to Claytor Lake, you asked me about Connor. I told you I missed him terribly since I had to leave him behind in the Aboves."

I nodded, hoping nothing bad had happened to her son.

She continued, "And then you announced in the Senate that you wanted my son as well as your family to be able to come to Seneca."

"Yes, I remember."

"Doro, I let you believe Connor was my son because that was what you thought when I was talking about him. My intention was to give you something that would make our experiences relatable… but…"

"Why, is he not your son?"

"Connor is my nephew. He's my brother's son."

I squinted, taken aback.

"There's no excuse. It was wrong and I know it. I want to make it right."

I replayed our flighter ride, recounting the moment when she let me believe something that she knew wasn't true, and I wondered why. I felt my body begin to react, like a vomit reflex was coming on, and in an instance I stopped it. I looked at Ellen. The past wasn't in front of me. She was.

"Well, thank you," I said, and I truly felt a sense of forgiveness.

I could tell Ellen was struggling because I had never seen her challenged to speak like this. It was obvious this wasn't about me or my reaction. She hadn't forgiven herself. She'd held on to this. She wanted to say more. It took her a second, but she finally did. "I lost both of my parents when I was in my twenties. My brother and I grew apart after we lost them. He never accepted the choices I made and my line of work, so I barely ever got to see Connor. I loved him and I tried to be there, but my brother didn't want me coming in and out of Connor's life the way I was. He was protecting him. I get it. I never got married because I couldn't ever put the stress of my confidential life on someone else. I never got to experience the kind of connection that you and Dom have, and if I ever began to, I had to squash it."

"That's awful, Ellen. I can't even imagine."

"It has been a challenge, but nothing is permanent."

Ellen studied my face and I think she became relieved to see I wasn't upset with her, but also to have that heavy load off her chest. It showed such humility that she could say that stuff to me, and so I realized, yet again, just how much I admired Ellen.

"I'm glad I met you, Ellen."

Ellen smiled. I hugged her and said, "I can see why they say, *'Friends are the family you choose.'*"

# 12

IDLE HANDS WERE not in my repertoire. My mom's disappearance gnawed at my gut, kicking my action mode into high gear. With tomorrow consumed by the Mars intel mission, I had to act now. After a frustrating game of flex tag, I headed to her residence. Of course, she wasn't there. Killer barked like a madman from the other side of the door. As much as I wanted to scoop him up, I had to keep moving.

I flexed my mom again, my stomach twisting as I placed a trace on her flexer. Invading her privacy made me sick, but enough was enough. Her location pinged back, and I set off.

Near the fitness zone, I spotted her. Hooded sweatshirt, black baseball cap, and stretchy workout pants—it was a bizarre incognito getup, like she was a celebrity dodging paparazzi. Aerobic exercise wasn't her thing. My mom hiked and did yoga, not spin. Why was she pedaling on a bike?

She could work out, but she couldn't call me back?

Frustration flared as I debated confronting her or flexing to see if she'd ignore it. Before I could make a decision, a tall black man in a black track suit and cap stepped onto the bike next to her. He twisted slightly, and spoke to her in a whisper. My stomach dropped as I caught the sharp edge of his goatee. Lieutenant Otis. Gregory Zaffron's superior. The man who'd threatened me after the nanobot hack. Why was my mom talking to a S.O.I.L. officer?

She waved her wrist at Marcus, her eyes flashing with anger. The sleek, advanced flexer on her wrist caught my attention—it wasn't the traditional model she'd worn for years. My stomach churned at the sight. This wasn't just an upgrade; it was something else entirely. I couldn't hear their conversation, but her expression said enough: she was furious and trapped. If he was monitoring her through that flexer, he wasn't just a threat to her. He was coming for me.

I edged closer, heart hammering. Without my flex implant, I had no FlexOculi scan to rely on. I'd have to spy the old-fashioned way. My fingers fumbled with my flexer, tuning it as a makeshift sound amplifier.

"You think I need a leash?" she spat, glaring at him. "She's my daughter, Marcus. My responsibility. Not yours."

"She's a liability, Nora. Don't let your emotions blind you to that." He gestured toward the flexer now strapped around her wrist. "You'll thank me when this keeps her safe."

Her laughter was bitter. “Safe? This isn’t safety. It’s surveillance.”

“This is how the game is played.”

“I want nothing to do with it. I just want my family back.”

“Well, maybe this reunion was not your smartest decision, Nora.”

*Nora.* There it was again. First Ellen, now Lieutenant Otis.

“You know I’m not here to cause problems.”

“Nobody forced your hand. You signed off on this. We gave you everything you asked for.”

She laughed, a dry, bitter sound. “Let’s be real. This didn’t exactly follow the script.”

“Does it ever?”

“I just want answers.”

“I don’t blame you. But you know how information works here.”

“If it means pulling me back in, so be it. Protecting my family is non-negotiable.”

“You know I can’t do that.”

Her voice tightened like a clenched fist. “I gave my life to the agency. Even now, the agency still has me by the throat. I’ve stayed quiet, minded my own business, didn’t ask questions when my husband disappeared. I let my daughter come here, for

God's sake!"

"I appreciate the sentiment, Nora. We all get emotional about loved ones."

"Emotions? This isn't about emotions. These are real lives, Marcus. *She's a child.*"

"If you want this conversation to continue, drop the theatrics."

She exhaled, the fire in her eyes dimming. "Fair enough." A pause. "Please, just cut the crap. It's me, Marcus. Not some stranger."

"That's exactly why you should trust that every decision we make is grounded in the intelligence and principles we both stand for."

Her pedaling slowed. She was out of breath, but not from the exercise. Eyes squeezed shut, she seemed on the verge of breaking. "My daughter almost died, and you want me to *rest*?"

My flexer blared suddenly, the opening riff of Michael Jackson's 'Thriller' shattering the tension. My stomach flipped. They both turned. I ducked behind the wall, scrambling to silence it. Static crackled, then nothing. When I peeked back, Marcus was gone. My mom pedaled furiously, her glare fixed straight ahead, as if the conversation had never happened.

I returned to session with a leaden pit in my stomach. Cramps gnawed at my side as thoughts swirled. My mom was healthy and pedaling a bike, sure, but that wasn't enough to reassure me. Now I, also, knew too much—but not enough.

My mom's connection to this deceptive world was deeper than I'd realized. Layla Campbell wasn't just a nurse scraping by with barista shifts. She was part of the system that stole my dad from our family. She had a history as tangled and complex as the code running the interplanetary bots. And somehow, she'd kept it from me.

# 13

MY APPETITE WAS shot. The revelation that my mom was involved with these higher-ups churned my stomach like heavy cream into butter. Each thought of food threatened to unleash a dry heave. How could *she*—my mom—live with this deception? An oath to the same agency that vanished my dad and nearly destroyed me? This was a sucker punch to the gut. But I couldn't spin out. Not now. Too much was at stake.

I grabbed an apple, chomping down the juicy nutrients to fend off blood sugar chaos, and headed to meet my crew.

We needed the full picture of Seneca's Mars plan. There were layers of intel to uncover: the training programs, the departure process, the tech millions of miles away. Mars departure simulations were a part of the groundwork for interplanetary migration, showcasing the extensive preparation required. Ellen had FigureFlex clearance for the Mars training facility in Australia—our ticket to gathering intel without setting off alarms. The simulations only happened the first Saturday of every month. This weekend was our shot. Dom, Ellen, Shields, and I agreed to meet after session to finalize our plan.

In the meantime, I headed to the S.E.R.C. lab and convinced a skeptical Yoshi to join the mission. The promise of controlling a bot on Mars had been too tempting for him to refuse.

The plan was simple but hardcore. During the FigureFlex simulation, I'd plant malware on the bots. Once back, Yoshi would help me tap into the bot network, translating their feedback as I dug deeper. We'd map the network, trace the commands, and unravel who was pulling the strings. It wasn't rocket science. It was way more complex—and totally my jam.

Late that Saturday morning, we gathered in Professor Shields's Ethics room. He locked the door. "Alright," he said. "We're set."

I scrambled our flexer signals, making them appear scattered across the hub—a basic hack, nothing too complex. The hub's tracking systems would pick up phantom pings, sending their operators on a wild goose chase. Just enough time to do what came next, which wouldn't be so elementary.

We synced our flexers—wearable neural interfaces designed for high-fidelity group immersion—and connected for a joint FigureFlex session. As the link activated, my vision shimmered, and the world around me dissolved into the grid of the Mars training facility's server.

Shields guided us in, his avatar sharp-edged and glowing faintly with the facility's virtual parameters. Ellen took point, and she led us through the simulation's launch bay. The rocket simulator materialized ahead: stark and utilitarian, all steel grates and exposed rivets. It wasn't the glossy, commercialized spacecraft of the Blue Origin era—this was raw, industrial functionality, built for survival and mechanics, not showmanship.

"Okay," Ellen warned, "try not to get sidetracked. We only have two minutes with the bots."

"It's crazy how ready I feel when I have no idea what to expect."

She smiled. "Confidence suits you."

"Learned it from you."

"And now I'm learning from you." Her words echoed in my mind as a silky voice filled the chamber:

*Activate Mars Departure Simulation.*

The vessel vibrated, my ears tingled. Ellen saw me as a partner now, not just a student. The thought warmed me even as the world turned black.

*Welcome, Citizens. We begin your departure experience today with a reminder of how far we've come—and how much further we will go.*

The voice wove through the darkness, painting human

history in poetic sweeps. Ants on a rock hurtling through space. Civilizations built and destroyed. Mountains cut by roads, plains crowned with skyscrapers. Flesh to dust. Hearts to memory. Each breath washing away into the past like dust in the wind.

*Hand-in-hand, we look forward. In the calm after the storm, we see clearly: dismal is as fleeting as a flat Earth. We relight the torch of exploration and migration. It was only a matter of time before we became interplanetary nomads... and that time is now.*

*This is Seneca Evolution.*

The screen bloomed with a powder-blue sky.

*Brace yourself for take-off. Two hundred and fifty million miles beyond Earth lies our new home. Mars.*

The countdown began.

*10... 9... 8...*

My heart pounded.

*4... 3... 2... 1...*

*Lift off!*

G-force crushed me, teeth digging into the inside of my mouth, skin stretched taut. I reminded myself my body was safe in Seneca, but anxiety rattled my bones. Stars streaked by in glowing torrents. The farther we traveled, the more natural it felt. Unease slipped away, replaced by a serene hunger for discovery.

*This simulation compresses the one hundred and twenty days of Departure into mere minutes. Early settlers will face danger. Trial and error. Fatalities. But with risk comes reward.*

A memory flared: Frank Wallingsford telling me that joining the Seneca Society meant leaving the Aboves forever. Some choices, once made, couldn't be undone.

*Your physical preparations and gene edits will sustain you on Mars—but returning to Earth carries a high risk of rapid degeneration.*

*Gene edits.* The words clanged like a warning bell. Would I need to be biologically modified to survive Mars?

*To protect our species in space, you will benefit from DNA edits and advanced biomedicine procedures. You will become a Seneca Sapien, adapted to thrive on a new terrain.*

My mind spiraled. Gene edits, computerized sight? What safeguards could I write to prevent someone from hacking my vision? But what if I could hack *theirs*? See across planets? The idea thrilled me and freaked me out simultaneously.

Creamy streaks of light burst through the darkness, then slowed to single stars. We entered a new phase of the journey. Goosebumps prickled my skin. My gut whispered that the real exploration—the real battle—was only beginning.

# 14

*After a period of travel, you will arrive on Mars. You will be surprised to see it does not appear red. This is because of the blue shield around the planet, created from Seneca's own proprietary Doromium. Please hold on securely as we initiate the landing sequence.*

The glowing purple sphere ahead swelled as we approached, and we plunged through the exosphere into Mars' cool atmosphere, the spacecraft's deep purr reverberating through my bones. It was the most powerful machine I'd ever experienced—yet I wasn't truly *in* it. The disconnect felt strange. I saw the effects of the simulation on others who couldn't see me, wrapped as we were in invisible flex.

We soared over a polar ice cap that sprawled beyond sight, a pristine expanse of white stretching endlessly, like a frozen Grand Canyon. Relief washed over me as we reached terrain marked by human innovation—buildings, satellites, roadways. The umber ground was speckled with the same marshmallow-colored domes I'd seen in the Australian training center. Thousands of people moved below with a synchronized purpose that outpaced even New York's busiest streets.

*Ladies and gentlemen, take a deep breath and behold our glorious new home.*

My virtual heart raced. Dom and I shared a bewildered glance, our 3D forms glitching slightly in the flex simulation. Even millions of miles away, his presence warmed me.

The spaceport below looked like something from antique comic book art—a utilitarian labyrinth of satellites and building-sized coils. As our virtual vessel touched down, my pulse pounded. This wasn't just a simulation; this was a step onto another planet's soil, an experience made real by technology.

Per the guide's directions, we followed the group onto a sleek Personal Flight Vehicle. As we lifted off, the host's voice filled the cabin:

*Mars is frigid, plunging to negative one hundred degrees Fahrenheit at night. Gravity here lets you jump over your car instead of walking around it. A day is thirty-nine minutes longer. The ninety-six percent carbon dioxide atmosphere is set to see the first steps toward transformation, with oxygen levels beginning to rise as terraforming efforts progress over the next decade.*

The information was dizzying and they just kept

delivering more details. Gene edits, Doromium shields, terraforming bacteria—all converging to remake a hostile planet into home. The ground swarmed with bots: hundreds, thousands, moving like an ant colony. Some marched in perfect lines; others paired off or went rogue, making decisions that seemed... autonomous.

"Okay, this is it, Doro," Ellen whispered. A ten-ton weight settled on my shoulders. "We have two minutes with the bots."

*Here, one of Seneca's largest robotic populations works to extract water from the soil, rich with usable ice and polymers for bricks.*

*One of.* The phrase thudded in my mind. This was just *one* unit of a robotic army numbering in the hundreds of thousands. What were the others doing?

Scientists in sleek, titanium-white suits worked alongside the bots. The bots' eyes—eerily human—caught my attention. Would we coexist with them someday? The thought was insane.

"Go time," I whispered, fingers wiggling to open a computing dock on my flexer. I captured images for Yoshi: bots marching like Soviet-era parades, pairs breaking formation to act independently. The host droned on about robotic efficiency, but I focused on my task: inserting the malware to decode this network.

*Seneca will be the first society with a one-to-one bot-to-citizen ratio. Imagine your own robotic butler.*

The idea of a butler bot was tantalizing, but now wasn't the time for daydreams. I sent commands, fast and furious. Each one returned gibberish. Nonsensical noise. Panic clawed at me. I tried again and again, my fingers a blur, but the feedback was garbage.

With twenty seconds left, self-doubt reared its ugly head. Who was I to think I could outsmart the architects of interplanetary tech? My heart pounded.

*Focus, Doro. Focus!*

I targeted the bot's motherboard—except there wasn't one. Nothing to hack. Five seconds left. I'd failed. I sank back, empty-handed and hollow. My confidence crumbled.

* * *

Back in session the next morning, Yoshi waited for me, arms crossed, robotic nostrils flaring. The ridiculousness almost made me laugh, but I didn't have a chuckle in me.

"Listen," I sighed. "It didn't go as planned. Give me a break."

"You did not keep your word."

"There was nothing to get."

"Nothing?" His eyes narrowed. "There is no such thing

as 'nothing' in bot language."

"Trust me. It was noise."

Yoshi snorted. "Give it here."

He scrolled through the gibberish. Professor Keatts began class, but Yoshi's face scrunched like a raisin.

"This is not noise," he muttered. "It is similar to Australian robotics code—but it is different."

"You can tell just by looking?"

He shot me a *duh* look.

"Right. Sorry."

"It needs to be broken down manually. It will take me time."

An idea struck. "What if you decode a few lines, and I write a program to analyze it against our bot language?"

His eyes lit up. "Now we are talking."

Hope flared. The chaos of techno-gibberish was hiding *something*. Yoshi's ridiculous humming and grunting was amusing, but the situation was dead serious.

My fingers itched. With my flex implant activated, this could be done in seconds instead of hours. All the computations, translations, and decoding—instantaneous.

And if Yoshi and I succeeded, I could speak directly to the bots.

I thought about choices. Simplicity. A life off-the-grid. But that wasn't why I'd been pulled back from the brink. The universe didn't bring me here to smell the roses.

It brought me here to fight.

# 15

I HADN'T BEEN back to C-QNCE since waking from my coma—if that's what you want to call it. The word "coma" made me shudder. That experience wasn't unconsciousness; it felt like the exact opposite.

That afternoon, my mom arrived at my place to take me to my neurological check-up with Dr. Cairncross. I planned to request my flex implant be reactivated to its pre-coma state. It struck me as odd that I hadn't heard from Dr. Cairncross since my near-fatal episode, but I checked myself—I wasn't the center of The Seneca Society. Dr. Cairncross was busy with consciousness research far beyond my understanding. She wasn't my personal nurse.

My mom, though, was a nurse. And apparently a CIA operative. Or something like that. She knew about the check-up, but the flex implant was another story. If she found out, she'd explode. Then again, maybe she already knew. Maybe she was keeping tabs.

One command in the BioNan, and my brain would rejoin the explosively expanding web of intelligence known as the grid. A simple decision with ultra-complex consequences. Instead of listing reasons not to, I focused on the pros:

One: Instant communication with others who had the implant. Two: Immediate computing and AI interaction—especially with Martian bots. Three: Access to my Veil, anywhere, anytime. Critical. When I was lost in Peru, I had to cut off Veil access after it was hacked. Before that, I relied on it like a superpower. My flex implant was the bridge between my mind and the information superhighway.

Then—boom—it was deactivated in C-QNCE, and I lost it all. Now I was about to get it back. But those abilities came with danger, some I couldn't even predict. I hesitated. Dr. Cairncross did, too. But she had to comply. She'd made the medical call to deactivate me, but since the implant was preexisting, she had to restore it.

I understood the risks. My heartbeat echoed in the dark BioNan chamber. With each beat, my dreams of a simple life slipped away. This wasn't for the faint of heart. If someone came for me in grid warfare, I'd do my best to take down the house.

I took a deep breath. Red light pierced through my eyelids. Electric beams danced across my cheeks. I braced for the cerebral flexes to flood in after so much time off-grid. The machine's soft whir drew me into a trance. Time slowed. My body glowed BioNan red.

I sensed someone—something—with me. Not the light sources from before I woke up in C-QNCE. Different. Wait—I wasn't asleep. The process was done. Seconds had passed—or maybe it was some kind of time trick.

The metal panel slid me out of the dark tunnel. The red beams vanished like figments of my imagination. Signals downloaded into my mind: messages, notifications, software updates. My FlexCore went wild with nutrition alerts. That familiar nudge to eat a banana ASAP. I welcomed the ease of flex-forward living, even knowing the chaos that came with it.

Dr. Cairncross hovered above me, eyes on the BioNan's 3D interface.

"What you're feeling is normal."

"Are you sure?" my mom asked, glancing between me, Dr. Cairncross, and the frantic data stream.

How did Dr. Cairncross know what I was feeling? Was she in my head? Did that mean that S.O.I.L. was here, too?

"Don't worry, I'm not reading your mind," she said. "I know this process like my ABCs. After the initial data surge, you'll compartmentalize. You'll control the flow soon. For now, let yourself acclimate."

I was back in the hyper-connected techno universe. But something was different. I had instant communication with everyone in my network—and they had access to me. My location, my connection. I hadn't updated my privacy settings yet.

*Doro!*

*Reba?!*

*It's been too long! Where are you?*

Dr. Cairncross shook my arm. "Doro? You okay? Talk to me."

"No—it's Reba!"

"Something's wrong," my mom said urgently.

Dr. Cairncross studied the screen, eyes narrowing as data cascaded.

"I'm monitoring," she said calmly.

"He's gone!" I gasped. "I can't reach him! Someone help us!"

"Hang in there," Dr. Cairncross said. "Your system is still rebooting."

"I'm not a system!" My voice cracked. "I'm human! My friend was just here!"

"Okay, Doro," my mom said gently. "I believe you. Breathe."

Dr. Cairncross leaned closer to the screen, her expression sharp. She waved two assistants over. The room blurred. My mom's face dissolved. And then—

Nothing.

# 16

I HAD A legit logical understanding of the importance of sleep for brain function, but that didn't mean I could click my heels together and fall into a slumber. My memory only replayed from the point where I got back to my mom's place. I was slightly delirious, nauseous as ever. That feeling where if you move a centimeter, you'll puke.

My mom said Dr. Cairncross would get back to us with the reasoning for the jumbled information when I got reactivated, after she figured it out. Signs firing off across the galaxy hinted that something sinister was brewing, and my mind spiraled in the perpetual hole of "what ifs." How could she not know?

I didn't want to sleep. I was waiting for my connection with Reba to kick back in. Finding clear headspace was impossible with my Veil bombarding me with nonstop information. Exhaustion rendered me wired. The could-puke-any-moment sensation mixed with the buzz of three cups of coffee on an empty stomach. Electricity hummed to my fingertips. I flung the covers off, curled into the fetal position, squeezed my eyes shut, and shook my hands, trying to purge the anxiety. I focused on my breath, my tight brow softening.

At some point, my body jerked and then shut down. I sank into the shallows of night.

*Hey chica.*

*Reba! Oh my god! There you are!*

*I've been with you all along, Campbella. Why ya so surprised?*

*I thought we got disconnected. I felt you communicating directly with me, but it wasn't like a flex. What was that? Please tell me what's going on!*

*When you reactivated your flex implant, you must have tapped into Seneca's Crystal Cloud.*

*Crystal Cloud? I don't get it.*

*You will. You connected with my synthetic consciousness. It felt like me because differentiating between truth and a computerized version of truth is a skill you need to refine.*

*Jeez, what does that even mean?*

*Now that you're in the Crystal Cloud, you'll need to master observing your mind—so you know which mind you're thinking with.*

*The Crystal Cloud? Is that where we are now?*

*You're there. But we're still our individual selves, too.*

*Okay, Reebs, seriously, you're trippin' me out.*

*I know it's confusing. Everyone in The Seneca Society is integrated into the Crystal Cloud somehow. Most just have one-way communication. You're hardwired—two-way street, sending and receiving.*

*Oh, great. Just what I need!*

Reba flex-laughed. His humor was a breath of fresh air.

*Why, though?* I thought. The answer came instantly—not from Reba, but from a gut feeling I couldn't explain.

*It's because...*

I felt his wheels turning.

*You tied the Martian bots to your flexer with malware. They're fueled by the Cloud's intelligence.*

*Oh no.*

*Oh yes. Like it or not, this is how the river flows. Jump in and learn to swim.*

*Story of my life.*

Reba laughed again.

*The Crystal Cloud, huh—do I even want to know what it is?*

He knew I did.

*They call it 'cloud consciousness,' but it's really automated decisions and near-perfect predictions based on cumulative data. 'Synthetic consciousness' is a misnomer. The Crystal Cloud is the most powerful algorithm—generating thoughts, decisions, communication—based on the collective mind of Senecans.*

It clicked. Superhuman capabilities.

*Yes. But superhuman capabilities don't beat the power of collective intuition.*

*So I tapped in and started getting premonitions. I knew I'd see you again. I have just been wondering where you'd been.*

*And here we are. Welcome to my world, Campbella. We've got both now. We need to know the difference and learn to operate in the space between.*

*Like psychic? Am I Intuerian, too, now?*

*Similar, but different. Trust that gut feeling. The Crystal Cloud updates you with data faster than you can say peanut butter. This is our evolution. Pay attention.*

A blaring alarm jolted me awake at 5:30 a.m. I gasped, rubbed my burning eyes, and blinked until my vision cleared. Squeezing my pillow, I wrestled with my body's urge to sleep. I needed to go back to the Cloud—to Reba. There were answers there. This wasn't a dream. It was another realm of reality.

But no time to snooze. Ellen, Professor Shields, Dom, and I had to meet Julian Hollenbeck at B3 Media before session. I pictured my mom at the doorway, urging me up. I was in her bed. She was probably on the couch. I dragged myself out of bed to check. Killer padded at my ankles.

My mouth brush cleaned my teeth, minty fresh, while

my brain sorted reality from the Crystal Cloud. Were we really converging with the bots? I spit, looked at myself in the mirror, and muttered, “Peeeanut butterrr.”

It hit me. I dropped onto my bed, retraced my flex archives, and connected the dots. A new line of automated communication flowed from my flex—straight to a quantum entangled network in Australia. The bots ran on Australian programming, too. We were all tied together. Me, Reba, the bots, and maybe two hundred thousand others.

Oh no. I was late for B3. I yanked on my S.E.R.C. blues and the boots from Dom’s store in New York, and bolted out the door—

*Not so fast, Campbella—*

Goosebumps prickled my arms. Reba’s warning echoed, but he wasn’t there. I froze, deja vu flooding me. I knew—somehow—I had one crucial move to make. Obvious, yet overlooked. The Crystal Cloud knew deeper. I needed quantum cryptography protection for all outgoing flex data. How would I even leave without it?

# 17

"SORRY, SORRY, JUST had to take care of something unexpected," I said as I rushed in, fifteen minutes late, sweat beads slipping down my hairline. My heart thumped so loudly I wondered if everyone else could hear it. They were all waiting for me at the acoustic carrier stop.

"We need to make up for lost time so we don't inconvenience Julian Hollenbeck," Professor Shields said, his tone even. Apparently, this crew wasn't suffering from a sleep deficit like I was. I plastered on a strong face, and we set off.

My adrenaline ebbed and I slipped into a zone as we glided along. The acoustic carrier moved smoothly, powered by sound waves we couldn't hear. The tech reminded me of Seneca's genius—and the rides I'd taken with Dom, who now had his arm around me. Ellen, on my other side, tucked her chin down and sent me a flex.

*You okay?*

*I don't know about okay, but I'm here.*

*Let me know if anything feels off.*

*Everything feels off.*

*Touché.*

The carrier came to a stop. The doors opened, and we stepped into the lobby of a grand media center. Screens blazed with color and motion. People hustled in all directions, cups in hand—coffee, brain-boosting brews, and who knows what else. Conversations hummed with energy. Shields led the way; he'd been here before.

A screen showing the Mars training facility bots snagged my attention. Then, a burst of blue on the next screen pulled my eyes to the Doromium project in Peru. Another screen panned across fields of cultivated greens, narrated by B3's star reporter, Becky Hudson.

Was she here now? I wondered. This place was the heart of Seneca's news and media. I'd seen B3 News everywhere—from the carrier to my room to the South American hub. Their broadcasts covered everything: climate devastation in the Aboves, the flighter crash months ago when G.W. took us to that Georgetown party. The sensory overload jolted my mind, scattering my thoughts. I needed to focus on the *now*—on making news, not reliving it.

"Mate!" A deep, enthusiastic voice boomed.

I turned to see Julian Hollenbeck's cleft-chinned, billion-dollar smile heading toward us, arms spread wide. Smile lines framed his eyes and mouth; his wavy hair was effortlessly perfect. His baby-blue button-up revealed a tuft of chest hair, a subtle badge of the middle-age heartthrob. He hugged Shields, while a poised, Middle-Eastern-looking woman, maybe twenty-five, approached us.

"Hi, I'm Julian's assistant, Rana."

We introduced ourselves. The lack of pretense eased my nerves. Shields and Hollenbeck knew each other from co-chairing the S.E.R.C. scholars media group. These people felt like the right company to be in.

A flowing Doromium blue screen glowed on Hollenbeck's face, even tinting the whites of his eyes. For a data girl like me, the blue reflecting in his eyes was a divine sign.

"To what do I owe this honor?" Hollenbeck asked, his gaze warm and curious.

"Julian, you know Ellen Malone," Shields said, patting his back.

"Of course!" Hollenbeck shook Ellen's hand firmly.

"Thank you for having us on such short notice," Ellen said, her smile rivaling his.

"Ah, short notice is more fun than long. So, here we are."

Shields introduced me next. "This is Doro Campbell, star S.E.R.C. scholar and daughter of Johnny Campbell."

"Nice to meet you, Mr. Hollenbeck," I said.

"Makes me sound ancient. Call me Julian."

I beamed and nodded. For a man who was once the world's richest and the founder of the largest media empire ever, he was surprisingly down-to-earth—just like the rumors said.

"And who's the lucky guy?"

Dom confidently extended his hand. "I'm Dominic Ambrosia, sir."

"Great handshake, Sir Dominic."

Julian looked around. "Let's skip the small talk, shall we?"

He turned to Rana. "Studio Five?"

"It's clear," she confirmed.

"Perfect." He nodded down the hall, and we followed Rana into the studio. Lights powered on, illuminating the empty stage and equipment.

"Water or tea?" Rana offered.

"Tea, please," I said, and everyone else echoed.

We gathered around a table where a mechanical pot poured steaming tea into five cups. Rana served us with a steady hand.

Seeing a real TV studio in person was mind-blowing. But then my stomach dropped. A mannequin-like Becky Hudson sat propped in a reporter's chair at the desk in front of a green screen.

Dom and I locked eyes, the same realization hitting us.

"Julian, is that a bot version of Becky Hudson?" I asked.

"This *is* Becky Hudson."

"Where's the real one?" A gut-churning dread settled in. There was no real Becky Hudson. Reba's warning buzzed in my mind: *pay attention.*

Julian's answer was casual. "The engineers and programmers who run her aren't on schedule right now."

Ellen and Shields didn't even flinch. They knew.

Julian sat on the stage floor and waved us over. I positioned myself to keep an eye on the bot.

"Becky Hudson," Julian said proudly. "Designed in my daughter's likeness. Bloody cool, isn't she?"

"Mmm hmm," I murmured, torn. "I guess that's the perfect segue into why we're here."

Julian's eyes sparkled. "I reckoned this was a visit of substance."

Over the next hour, we laid everything out: nanobots in bloodstreams, the manipulation of my dad's mind for control of Doromium, the Departers' plan to colonize Mars, and B3 Media's role in spreading propaganda. Julian listened intently. Rana stayed composed, but anger simmered behind her eyes.

"My friends," Julian finally said, his smile tempered by gravity. "I got into this business to seek and expose truth. Like attracts like, and here we are. This is the most important information ever to cross my desk."

Relief washed over me. Coming to him had been the right call—but not the final move.

"And while we watch this play out, free will is at stake," Shields added.

"But we won't just watch," Dom insisted.

"Can you help us?" I asked, hope clinging to my words.

"My job is to deliver information impartially. But what people do with it—that's out of our hands. Controlling that outcome would make us no better than the Departers."

I looked at Dom. Sadness flickered in his eyes. But I knew what I wanted: for people to have a choice, for Doromium to heal Earth, and for my family to be whole again.

Shields nodded. "We have to trust that humanity's best interests will prevail."

"Exactly," Julian agreed. "It won't be easy, but we bend toward justice… and morality."

Dom scratched his chin. "It's still confusing. Why support Mars exploration if it doesn't benefit both sides?"

"It's mutually beneficial," Julian explained. "Flex Corp controls the software—nanobots, flex networks. SGE Corp controls the hardware—Doromium, Mars bots. They both profit because mankind is the ultimate asset."

"This is why we're here," I said.

Julian nodded. "To inform, educate, and maybe even

entertain again someday. But for now, the fight's a game of chess, not a boxing match."

Everyone agreed.

"With B3's global reach, billions will hear your truth. And I bet they'd rather not lose free will."

Ellen cleared her throat. "We need to be ready. There will be repercussions."

And we were ready.

# 18

AFTER THAT BRAINSTORM bender of insane proportions, I craved a blissful dinner at Ty Sakai's. The thought of melt-in-your-mouth halibut cheek made my stomach groan. I couldn't silence the beast, and the trademark fresh-cut watermelon scent of the restaurant didn't help.

Seated at the sushi bar of my dreams, I demolished a bowl of sticky rice drenched in hot sauce, just to calm my hunger enough to function like a human. Ty, the masterful itamae, was already slicing magic.

"There she is!" Ty's pep shot through me like a sunbeam. He was a friend far removed from Senecan politics and corruption. Here, in his culinary domain, flavors ruled—and life felt simple.

"What's up, Ty?" I asked, grinning.

"Slicin' and dicin'! Where's my boy?"

"He had errands, but he'll be here soon."

Ty nodded and sent out the plate of halibut cheek I'd dreamed about. In my nightmares, the plate passed me by, but not today. Today, at least one bite was mine. Chilled perfection, two inches away from bliss.

Before I could taste it, a voice whispered near my ear, hot breath prickling my skin. "Stay calm. Don't act surprised to see me."

I turned to see a pair of deep-green eyes. It was Jadel—the Afro-Brazilian, undercover S.O.I.L. operative who'd saved me in Peru! Memories of him sneaking me into the South American Hub jolted me. He wasn't here for sushi.

Keeping my face neutral, I whispered, "What are you doing here?" Then I shoved the halibut into my mouth before the chance slipped away. You never knew what was next with Jadel.

"S.O.I.L. has been tracking your every step."

"Not surprised," I said, bracing for more.

Since my NeuroQuE experience, Dom and I had cautiously gathered intel. Bringing Professor Shields and Julian Hollenbeck into our circle was a risk, but necessary. My gut told me they were the right allies: one with knowledge of society, the other with media.

The halibut cheek disintegrated on my tongue, a burst of citrus magic. My eyes closed, and I nearly purred.

"That looks good," Jadel said.

"Good? Jadel, this is *beyond* good. Bummer you don't

have Ty's in Hub 48." I pushed my plate toward him, pitying his rubbery river snail diet.

"Food is for function, not fun."

"For someone as intelligent as you, that's an incredibly dumb take," I shot back. "Life's meant to be enjoyed, especially when S.O.I.L. could take me out at any moment."

"Fair enough."

"This is something you need to try before you die." I framed the fish like the Mona Lisa.

Jadel picked up a piece of kumquat sushi. The second it hit his tongue, he froze. His eyes popped open like he'd been electrocuted, then slid shut, savoring the flavor.

"You are a smart one."

"Ty's the smart one," I replied, noticing Ty watching us.

Time to move before anyone got curious. Jadel and I left the restaurant district, hopped onto the acoustic carrier, and rushed down the aisles until we found an empty car. He slid into a seat. I dropped beside him.

"I will make this quick and go," he whispered.

"Go where?"

"Back."

"You came all this way for one conversation?"

"Some moments are more important than the distance."

I smirked. "Big talk for a shady S.O.I.L. character."

"I may work undercover, but knowing your dad and his

intentions with Doromium changed my loyalties. Call it 'shady,' but I've made thoughtful decisions."

"So you're a double agent."

"Labels are dangerous."

"Well, that's what you are."

"Technically, yes. I was inducted into Seneca from the CIA, assigned to serve Seneca's power players while feeding intel back to the Agency. But then came your father, Doromium —and you."

"Me?"

"Yes. Information in Seneca is controlled and compartmentalized. My mission was to protect your life. The more I learned about you and the mission, the clearer the deeper purpose became. Before I could fully understand it, you left."

"And my dad asked you to babysit me."

Jadel sighed. "Do you always jump to conclusions?"

He had a point. I replayed his words and put myself in check. *Do not assume.* Collect data. Let the truth reveal itself—just like Reba suggested.

"After you left," Jadel continued, "I dug into the players: Ellen Malone, Senator Gilroy, the Wallingsfords… your mom."

"My *mom*?!"

"I tracked meetings, locations, financial trails. Your dad has access to it all. The agenda is clear: control Earth's resources. Doromium is key."

"I know." He wasn't telling me anything new.

"But intelligence knows that *you* know."

My stomach dropped. "How?"

"Good question."

"Why haven't they stopped us if they're so aware? S.O.I.L. always shuts down threats."

"They're observing you. Watching your moves, your assets, your plan. You're in the tunnels; they're above, watching. They want to know everything before they strike."

"Who? How? Our circle is tiny."

"But a few of you know too much."

"Yeah, me and—" I stopped, thinking I could protect Dom by keeping quiet.

"Dominic Ambrosia," Jadel said smoothly. "Where did he go while you were with Higashi, the robotics boy?"

Dom's voice came from behind us. "I was spreading our intel across a web of vaults. If someone comes for us, our work won't disappear."

# 19

I SPUN AROUND to see Dom walking towards us, nostrils flaring, jaw clenched, eyes pinned on Jadel. His voice was deep and resolute. "So you should know, you try anything crazy right now, it won't do you any good. The intel is out there."

Jadel remained remarkably calm, not moving an inch. "Mr. Ambrosia."

"Stand up and back away from my girlfriend."

"Take a breath." Jadel smiled.

I had to interject before this escalated. "Dom, this is Jadel. He came on behalf of my dad."

My words didn't seem to affect Dom. He was seething, testosterone cranking—and then he lunged at Jadel. Without hesitation, Jadel jabbed the tips of his fingers into the crease between Dom's neck and shoulder. Dom let out a strangled cry and crumpled to the floor of the acoustic carrier, pain contorting his features.

"Dom!" I yelled, diving next to him. Jadel remained motionless, his expression infuriatingly serene. I shot him a 'what the heck?' look. He shrugged. "What, did you want me to wrestle him?"

Dom lunged again, but I yanked him back. "Dom, stop!"

Jadel's faint smile returned. "She's right, you should stop. And while you're seated like a good boy for story-time, I have one for you."

"Screw you, dude," Dom snapped, standing up.

"I suggest you don't make any more silly moves, because next time I won't be so nice."

"That was nice?" I scowled at Jadel, holding tightly to Dom's arm.

"It was your sense of rebellion that got you into Seneca in the first place," Jadel continued. "Same with Doro. Same with me. In a way, we're all cut from the same cloth."

Dom stretched his neck. "What do you know about what got me in here?"

"The molecular biological system to trace and control the migration of whales—very impressive. No wonder S.O.I.L. wanted your technology… and you."

Dom squinted and took a seat across from Jadel, rubbing the sore spot on his neck. I knelt between them, ready to intervene before things escalated again.

Jadel leaned back. "Ever wonder what they did with

your mind's work? How they took your passion and twisted it for power? Like they did with Doro's dad, the master mathematician?"

Dom's forehead tightened, frustration burning in his eyes. He pressed his palms to his temples, trying to unlock a memory buried deep within his mind. I could feel his fierce desire for answers, blazing through the air and into my chest.

"Don't you wonder why dismantling the invasive nanotechnology in Operation Crystal came so naturally to you?"

Dom squeezed his eyes shut, straining to grasp something just out of reach. His mind raced, synapses firing like a lightning storm.

Jadel knew more about us than I'd thought. But I wasn't guessing. This guy wasn't a double, triple, or quadruple agent. He was an ally standing before us, a trove of data we couldn't afford to dismiss.

Dom and I sat perfectly still, eyes locked on Jadel, waiting for more.

"You don't trust Ellen, and there's a reason. Do you want to know why?" Jadel asked.

"Tell me, please," Dom said, his voice taut.

Jadel opened his hand, revealing a crystal-clear pill. "So many questions you have can be answered by your own mind if you take this."

Dom scoffed, looking away. "You're crazy."

"What is it?" I asked.

"The antidote to the Cogniz-X memory blocker S.O.I.L. uses. It disintegrates the plugs they put in your memory storage."

My breath caught. "When I was introduced to Seneca, they told me if I chose to go back to the Aboves, they'd erase the entire 48-hour period of my introduction. With Cogniz-X."

Jadel nodded. "This antidote isn't from S.O.I.L. But I have it." He fixed his gaze on Dom. "If you want the truth, you take this."

Dom's eyes zeroed in on the pill, hunger for knowledge blazing in his expression.

"You don't know for sure," Jadel admitted, "but if I wanted you dead or drugged, don't you think it would have happened by now?"

The pill arced through the air, time stretching unbearably. Dom snatched it, holding his past and future between his fingers. I slid onto the seat next to him. "No matter what, I'm here."

Without a word, Dom dropped the pill onto his tongue and swallowed.

Silence filled the carrier. The seconds crawled. Each breath felt heavy and infinite. I watched Dom, hauntingly still, his pupils dilating and contracting erratically. My heart pounded as I braced for the unknown.

After three minutes, Dom's head sank. His chin touched

his chest. Then his head snapped back, his face twisted in anguish. "It was me," he whispered.

His eyes darted wildly, searching the floor, back and forth, up and down, his mind blazing through realizations. Then he looked at me, horror etched in his features.

"I knew how to dismantle the bots because my own mind created them. I was the architect of the real truth behind the Necrolla Carne Virus."

"No," I breathed. But denial was pointless. The truth punched me in the gut.

"I remember it," Dom said hollowly. "Ellen recruited me for my tracking tech in Japan. The same tech that got me in trouble is why they brought me here."

His shoulders collapsed. Sorrow poured over him in waves, and I felt it too, drowning in his guilt. I placed a hand on his trembling arm, helpless.

"They brought me in. Wallingsford. Lieutenant Otis…"

Jadel grunted at the name.

Dom's memories unfurled, clear and brutal. "Senator Gilroy…"

I froze. "What?"

"They knew. And Ellen knew. She restrained me while they gave me the Cogniz-X shot. She knew I was lost in the dark."

"Everything has a reason," Jadel said calmly.

"Ellen's actions may seem questionable, but past choices don't always define who we are."

Dom's voice was a deadpan whisper. "I don't play with cheaters."

Jadel's words cut sharp. "Look in the mirror."

"I was backed into a corner. It was do or die."

"Yes. Exactly."

The lights shut down, and the carrier stopped in total darkness.

"Doro?" Dom gasped.

I grabbed his hand.

"Jadel?" I called.

No reply.

Dom's hand trembled, volts of panic sparking into mine. Eight breaths. The lights snapped on.

Jadel had vanished.

# 20

I LAY IN bed worried sick all night. Instead of tossing and turning, I was frozen in place, rigid with fear. The stillness tightened around me, feeding the panic. Was this anxiety, or something S.O.I.L. inflicted? My head spun out of control—worried for Dom, worried for the state of life, worried about the shifting motives of those around me. Each breath came shallow and strained, making me dizzy. Doubt pressed in, smothering every shred of certainty.

Dom wanted to be alone, but I needed him with me. Why did he choose distance when we needed unity? Jadel had disappeared into the shadows, too. I was a lone wolf in this hurricane of thoughts, unable to imagine what Dom was enduring. The clearer the air and brighter the sun inside me, the more violent the outside storms seemed. I thought I had learned to trust myself, no matter what spiraled out of control. But it was all unraveling again, and I wasn't ready.

Learning that Brittany's dad was aware of the whole Necrolla Carne situation shook me to the core. Did she know, too? About Dom? About the Crystal Cloud? What secrets did she hold? And Lieutenant Marcus Otis—what did he know? Was my closest girlfriend in Seneca a mole?

I needed to talk to her. I fired off a flex.

Hey. Can we ride tomorrow morning? I could really use a friend.

She replied right away.

Hey! Yes! Meet me at 7.

Seven it was— but first, a night of elusive shut-eye. I burned with thoughts, tangled in covers that I tossed off and on, off and on. My mind wrestled with what I *thought* versus what I *should* think. Mostly, I just wished my eyes would grow heavy and take me to the non-thinking place.

Restless turmoil on a too-soft pillow. Yet, somehow, morning broke, and I found fleeting peace on Seneca's lush, green pastures. Brittany and I trotted on the horses, then slowed to an easy stride. The scent of the dewy grass tickled my nose, settled in my throat. My senses melted into the still life, as if I became part of it. Finally, some calm since that tense acoustic carrier ride with Dom and Jadel.

I closed my eyes, flashed back to my first time on a horse with Dom—tearing through the Virginia forest at full speed. Fear had knotted me then, the thought of surrendering control to a creature I'd just met. But Dom had helped me conquer that fear, nudging me to find the confidence to mount Buck. Now, I rode Athena with a sense of peace. I stroked her mane. Brittany smiled at me.

I didn't want to shatter the serenity, but my friction with Seneca's hidden woes boiled beneath the surface. I couldn't hold it back.

"I'm just going to cut straight to it," I said. "Which side are you on?"

"Side?" Brittany's eyes widened.

"Departers? Repairers?"

She shifted in her saddle. Prince, her horse, sensed her unease and grunted.

"Neither? Both?"

"Politicking like your dad—that's so unlike you."

"What's that supposed to mean?"

"You tell me."

"Doro, this is weird."

"What's weird is that your dad knows about the nanobot invasion—Necrolla Carne. He was there, Brittany. He knows."

She pulled back on Prince's reins. "Whoaaa."

I tugged Athena to a halt, turning her so we faced each other.

"Okay," Brittany said. "This feels like an attack. I've always been honest with you. I know about Departers and

Repairers because that's all my dad talks about. But a nanobot invasion? No way."

"You don't know?"

"No!" Her voice cracked.

I wanted to believe her. "How could you *not* know? You're a traverser. Your dad is in the thick of everything."

"I have no idea what a nanobot invasion even is, Doro. It sounds like sci-fi!"

"Serious?"

"Serious."

I scanned her eyes. "You really think your dad's a good man?"

"He is. He wants the best for everyone."

"Then why is he part of a government that allowed this?"

"What?! What about your dad?!"

"That's apples and oranges."

"Not really. If I've learned anything from politics, it's that you lose yourself if you stop paying attention to what matters."

"Funny you say 'pay attention.' Someone else important to me said that to me, too."

"It's true. Through it all, I *know* my dad has great intentions. He doesn't agree with every law, but that doesn't make him complicit. You can't blame him for everything that happens in a system he's part of. That's like blaming you for the flighter crash just because you were there."

I exhaled. I got what she was saying. Her words held confidence, the kind I always wished I had. Was my distrust twisting stories that weren't real?

"Is he playing both sides?" I asked. "Isn't he one or the other?"

"Things aren't black and white. He's not a Departer or a Repairer. He's a Hybrid. And so am I."

"Hybrid?"

"He believes in exploring the universe and repairing Earth. We don't have to abandon home to move forward."

I nodded, absorbing her words. Departers. Repairers. Hybrids. It all swirled in my mind.

"Doro," she said softly. "I've been surrounded by politics my whole life. When I met you, it felt *real*. I want to be honest. I'm not just a Hybrid in ideology. I've gone through gene editing to live on Mars. All the Senate families who opted for Departure did."

"Gene editing? Like choosing eye color?"

"It's way beyond that. You'll see. You'll get this choice, too. Stay as you are, or train and edit yourself to depart. Once you commit, that's it. It's about what the decision *means* to you."

After the ride, my mind somersaulted. Departers. Repairers. Hybrids. There were more paths than I'd seen. I couldn't box myself in, even if the people I loved did.

My brain recontextualized, like the Crystal Cloud and my growth processing together. I wanted Earth repaired, as Dad had always intended. But the idea of departure—evolution—intrigued me. My parents might not understand. They had their own reality tunnels, but I could see it.

Seneca was evolution. And if I didn't carve the path forward, someone else would.

# *21*

WE COLLIDED LIKE magnets, drawn together and spinning around each other, navigating chaos like it was instinct. The force of this galaxy swept me to places I'd never been. Given the chaos tearing through L.A. and Earth itself, outer space felt like the only escape for Dom and me. We had a chance to flee the toxicity and create a new life on the clean canvas of Mars. A whole new planet where we could lead the charge.

It was dinnertime when I stopped by Dom's place. I hadn't heard from him since Jadel's revelation. That was heavy for Dom to process, and I just wanted to be there. He hadn't done anything wrong, but guilt weighed on him anyway.

Dom let me in, and the door slid shut behind me. He was lying on his bed, facing away.

"Hey, you sleeping?"

"Just napping. I'm beat."

He rolled over. His face was drained, pale, dark circles

shadowing his eyes. The crashing weight of his recent revelations about being the architect of the Necrolla Carne vaccine, on top of endless taxing days, had worn him down. I sat beside him and laid down. As I nestled against his warmth, I tried to absorb his suffering. His deep breaths filled the space between us, making it hard for me to breathe. I felt his pain and reached for his hand, sweaty and warm. I pressed my face to his back.

"You okay, Dom?"

"Mmm hmm."

His heartbeat betrayed him. He wasn't okay, and every cell in me wanted to make things right.

"Let's leave this all behind," I whispered.

He swallowed hard. His silence felt like distance, even though we were wrapped around each other.

"I'll never stop you from doing what you need to do, but…"

He turned to face me, chin dipping to his chest, eyes closed. I traced my hands along his arms, desperate to soothe him.

"This isn't about politics, Dom. It's exploration—survival! Humans survived by migrating. A thousand years ago, America wasn't even on the radar. Imagine where we'll be a thousand years from now. We can—"

"Doro, I can't go."

"We don't have to go now, but—"

He choked back tears, his breaths ragged. I tilted my head to meet his gaze, but he wouldn't look at me.

I squeezed his arms. "Dom."

He opened his eyes, locking onto mine.

"I love you, Doro. You know that, right?"

"Of course I do. I love you, too. You're really making me worried right now." My insides spun.

"Okay. Stop for a second." I wasn't sure if I was talking to him or myself. My eyes darted, searching for answers that weren't there. Dom cupped my face, pulling my gaze back.

"I understand going to Mars is something you need to do."

"We can do it together. Why wouldn't we?"

"We've never talked about it until now."

"All this chaos of the Aboves—don't you want to bail? Start fresh?"

"All this chaos brought me back to my purpose. Faith. God…"

"You can have faith anywhere."

He shook his head. "Departing isn't the way forward for me. I need to stay."

My mind protested, but my heart made me pause. I listened to his truth.

"I have to clean up the mess I made with the nanos."

"None of that was your fault."

"I didn't know, but I do now. I have to help fix the mess I created. Earth is a gift. I can't abandon it—or the creatures near extinction. God's creatures. I have to help."

The thought of being separated by billions of miles weighed on me, a dread I couldn't shake. But I couldn't stay stuck here. I had the chance—and the responsibility—to be part of humanity's evolution. There had to be a way for us to go without Dom feeling like he was abandoning Earth. I muttered, "We can figure this out later."

The moment the words left me, I knew they were a lie.

*Figure this out now.*

The realization hit me like a self-flex—an intuitive force so strong it drew me closer.

"Doro, you okay?"

"I am, I am..." My eyes darted. Without doubt, I whispered, "Dom, this can't wait."

He narrowed his eyes. I closed mine, listening to the truth beyond me, within me.

Dom understood the biological data behind the Crystal Cloud's intelligence programs—the system he helped design. He understood it because he'd created it. The problem wasn't the technology or the data, but what people *did* with it. It was—and always would be—about choice.

"Dom, I have these capabilities because of your

technology. You put nanobots in whales to help them. Your intention was pure. Don't let anyone twist that or make you believe you need redemption."

He sighed. "So now what?"

"Now we face it. The tech was misused, but that's the past. We have to steer the next phase. If we don't…"

Dom nodded, finishing my thought. "All hell breaks loose."

# 22

"HURRY! PLEASE!" DOM shouted at the emergency medical crew who rushed me on a steel stretcher through the halls inside Claytor Lake's gargantuan hub. "We need Dr. Cairncross now!"

Strapped down and convulsing, my eyes darted wildly, as if trapped in a storm of panic. We reached the end of the shiny white hall. I knew it was the threshold to Dr. Cairncross's wing and that it would take her own approval for the doors to open. Beyond the border was that stone labyrinth with its seismic, modern machinery that helped facilitate the path of our evolution.

The doctors in C-QNCE tried to wedge between me and Dom as we neared the top-secret chambers, but Dom refused to let them steal even an inch from the space between us. His eyes blazed with desperation, and his voice cracked as he snapped, "Back up!"

None of the doctors in their pristine white or powder-blue lab coats dared touch Dom, but then two S.O.I.L. guards moved in towards us. Even though I tried to keep my focus on monitoring the outgoing messages—having set my flex to block actual EEG measurements with a mock seizure—I was inevitably drawn to the presence of the ominous men in blue. Like lines of code, the information surged through my veins:

One: My flex activity fooled everyone—except S.O.I.L. They weren't fooled because they were in the Crystal Cloud with me.

Two: They made the doctors around us scram. Nobody messed with S.O.I.L.

Dom and I were quietly shuffled by the two S.O.I.L. guards and closed inside the white, cube-shaped room that I vaguely remembered as a transitional area. It clicked in my gut that these guys were neither for us nor against us; they were there to maintain stability inside the hub. The reality was, I was all for that, too.

The only thing I could do in that moment was ask them to turn around and make sure we were secured in the C-QNCE chamber. Before I had a moment to think, my conscious mind had extrapolated from the Crystal Cloud how to build a reason-based connectivity with the computerized intelligence in my presence. Meanwhile, Dom was a stone-carved version of himself, like a Civil War statue; engaged in war but frozen in time. He was concocting danger in his mind and his body was reacting in fear. The reality hit deeper for me. I knew this was unfolding just as it was supposed to.

The door to the main hallway slid shut behind the S.O.I.L. guards. Dom exhaled sharply, and I managed a weak smile. A second door shimmered open. Dr. Cairncross appeared, her baby-blue lab coat as crisp as ever. Without a word, she beckoned us in and moved to her BioNan monitor, her presence commanding the room.

The surrounding doctors jostled for her attention, barking facts at her a mile a minute. She seemingly absorbed the information overload but had something more concerning in her ether and so she dismissed them, "Very well, I'll take this from here."

With those words and one sweeping glance to everyone, the doctors and technicians cleared, no questions asked. Impressive.

Dr. Cairncross took a deep breath and said, "Follow me." Dom pushed my stretcher behind Dr. Cairncross, and she took us to an obsidian-black doorway on the stone wall.

Dr. Cairncross put her hand to a panel next to it, causing a thin line of electric blue light to outline the doorway's edge, tracing a precise, steady pattern. A charged stillness filled the space, sharp and metallic, like the moment before a storm breaks.

Without warning, the surface of the door rippled, a wave

of silver light passing across it. Then it split open down the center, edges folding away like liquid metal, disappearing into the walls with a whisper. The space beyond opened into a vast, domed C-QNCE chamber. The ceiling was a living canvas of holographic constellations, shifting and flowing in intricate, ever-changing patterns. The walls curved seamlessly into the floor, creating the sensation of standing inside a giant, illuminated neural network.

Tiny nodes of blue and violet light were interconnected along the walls, spreading into complex, organic pathways. The air was cool, but the energy in the room elicited a sense of infinite potential compressed into a single space. A faint vibration emanated from the floor, like standing on the edge of a bass speaker mid-rumble. In the center of the chamber, a raised platform shimmered, its surface fluid and reflective, morphing into whatever interface the mind required. Above the platform, a translucent orb hovered, swirling with flecks of gold and deep indigo—the crystallized intelligence of the Crystal Cloud, the very core of Seneca's quantum consciousness research.

"I knew you'd be coming," Dr. Cairncross said.

Lost in my head, I stammered for words. "I'm sorry, but I didn't have any other way to get in touch with you without going through Ellen or—"

"Do you know how many resources were pulled just now?"

The second she asked me, I actually knew the precise answer. What a trip. While she was unstrapping me from the stretcher, I zoned out for a second before noticing her and Dom waiting for me to speak.

"I promise we wouldn't have done this if it wasn't important."

Dr Cairncross looked apprehensively with her nose turned up at Dom. I could tell his anxiety was thrashing on the inside as he gnawed his cheek and furrowed his brow. "You know about the nanobots hidden in the Necrolla Carne vaccine, don't you?"

Dr. Cairncross studied Dom's demeanor as if she was reading it for a story other than the one he was telling. He swayed like he was about to pass out. I sat up from the stretcher and put my hand on his shoulder.

He continued quietly, "We both know what they were used for—"

I added, "*And* what they are used for now."

Dr. Cairncross put her hands together in a prayer pose below her sternum. "It isn't wise to bring this here."

Dom blurted, "I was the developer of the nanobots, and now we know they're being used to pull intelligence from all of us in Seneca to fuel artificial intelligence on Mars."

Dr. Cairncross had no reaction and my concern was growing. "Dr. Cairncross, you told me you had my best interests in mind."

"I do," she replied, her voice even.

"And your own? Do you know what they're using your work for?"

Her eyes narrowed. "I'm a scientist, not a politician."

I met her gaze. "In Seneca, everyone is a pawn, whether we know it or not."

Dr. Cairncross nodded, still unfazed. "Truly, I appreciate that in your youth you are so inspired. There is a dire importance for passion in a burgeoning society, but my place here is to work on the advancement of intelligent systems to benefit us as a species, not combat inevitable societal institutions."

"But what if your work is being manipulated to benefit those powerful institutions and build them up bigger and badder than ever instead of benefitting humanity as a whole?" I asked.

"That *is* what's happening," Dom said.

I didn't think Cairncross was privy to the big picture. As I had understood, information was compartmentalized, confined and manipulated. She needed to know more so we could, too.

I told her, "The Martian bots were communicating in programing lingo derived in Australia, but when we tried to access those coordinates, I found that the network was encrypted so hardcore that it would take a hacker a thousand years to break into it. I mean, there was no way. It *would* have been mathematically impossible *unless* I used the intelligence of the

Crystal Cloud to get in."

I could see Dr. Cairncross's wheels turning, which in turn triggered mine to accelerate at a mind-blowing speed. As Cairncross and Dom dialogued, I tuned out of the sound and went inside to tap into this instant intuit. I harnessed a deep understanding that Dr. Cairncross was not interested in doing her job in order to satisfy a moral compass. She was one hundred percent seeking meaning and purpose in the field in which she had risen to great success.

I paddled deeper inside the motherboard. Specifically modeled off of the top echelon of human intelligence and behavior, but with a near perfect memory, the Crystal Cloud was the convergence of the data of the greatest minds. From where I swam inside this space, I had an acute realization that *I* was the product of the goal. I couldn't fight it now, because I was it. Here was a creation humans always dreamt of bringing to fruition—to give life-like qualities to robots. But by merging myself with it, and giving AI capabilities to my human self, what would that mean to have the kind of power I had now? It was in my hands to regulate the balance between my humanity and machine intelligence.

"The Crystal Cloud has given the bots the intelligence of living beings. So robots are going about their business with free will to make decisions to problem solve. They can be snapped back into shape with overriding controls of the Cloud. So there becomes power over consciousness, and who has that power? Specific people with specific goals who are running this entire simulation," I told her.

"Yes, I understand." She said as if this was not news to her.

"The bots are under the control of S.O.I.L., who is under the control of Flex Technology Corporation," I added.

"I am aware."

"You're playing God," Dom snapped.

Equally as stern, Dr. Cairncross quipped back, "Nobody here is *playing* God. We are architects."

"Bullocks," Dom said facetiously. I wished he could just bite his tongue, but that wasn't Dom.

"Dominic, *if* we were created in the image of God, it has been hardwired in us to create inside this data and matter playground we've been given."

"This isn't a game, Doctor," Dom snapped, his hands shaking. "We're talking about the sanctity of life."

"The machines are not alive, they are a technology we have built to advance and benefit our own lives. Couldn't it then be considered that, in the spirit of the sanctity of life, it is worth making these breakthroughs for the enhanced wellbeing of billions of people?"

I agreed with both of them but knew something had to give when it came to overarching control.

"Okay," I said, "but we're in a dangerous space, Dr. Cairncross. *Yes*, the Martian bots are machines that learn, think and reason like people, developing at a pace set into motion long ago. *Yes*, this can help us. But this intelligence isn't predictable because real people aren't predictable, so as they continue to develop rapidly based on human brain logic and so on, they become increasingly unpredictable in *their* development. Not only that, but the powers-that-be control when and where that unpredictability will be unleashed."

I wondered. Dr. Cairncross's points were valid, but had she ever traveled beyond the field of thinkingness and felt what I felt when my body was left on that table and I had seen everything that was far outside of it?

"I think what Dom's concern is, isn't the whole point that the spirit—or soul—is something bigger than this?" I asked, "And how do we honor that?"

"Mm, hmm," Dr. Cairncross posed the rhetorical, "why all the dedication to the advancement of human intelligence, and not the heart of who we truly are as humans?"

I nodded, "The way Dom sees it is that our human nature has escaped us. Are we digging a deeper hole for ourselves that we might not ever be able to climb out of?"

Dr. Cairncross smiled. " I understand your concerns and appreciate that you're asking the hard questions. With every new technology comes a new controversy loaded with ethical debates that see no conclusion. These issues used to be confined to science fiction narratives or hypothetical conversations at the dinner table, but as the singularity between man and technology is no longer theory but reality, here we are, so now what?"

"Exactly!" I said.

"The point is *here we are*. The magnitude of artificial intelligence doesn't discount any force that may precede it. The idea of consciousness, the soul, higher beings, dare I say *God*, are differing components of this vast universe inasmuch as a human is different than a car, or a tree different than gravity. A leaf may fall from a tree branch to the ground because of the physics of gravity, but the two are not one and the same. Cutting down a tree does not destroy gravity just as building synthetic cloud consciousness does not destroy a soul."

"You've lost me," Dom said, but I could tell he wanted to understand.

He began pacing, which caused me to shift around, too, almost mirroring his moves.

"Our bodies are made of quarks and electrons, which follow the laws of physics. If the soul exists, it doesn't directly affect those particles—they operate independently. Think of your mind like a processor, Dorothy. You as a CPU, if you will. My work in C-QNCE is about integrating information, not tampering with the soul. We're expanding consciousness, not replacing it."

I nodded and looked to Dom. He squinted and nodded

lightly back to me and I saw it was clicking for him, too.

"Now imagine that information shared and processed with millions of other CPUs, allowing your single experience to be one of information integration—or, a higher level of consciousness. Now, I don't claim to have a doctorate in theology by any means, but lets hypothesize. *If* there is a soul, would it not benefit from such information integration?"

I asked, "But if our consciousness is still in the infancy stages of scientific research, how can it be synthesized?"

"Who said anything about infancy?"

Cairncross was right. What I felt inside was no infant situation. This had nothing to do with artificial intelligence. The morals in question are those that we try to assign and project onto technology by our own beliefs and actions, but the bottom line was that, one way or another, people would continue to evolve by technological and biological advances, and a slightly different sort of human will one day exist. I was well on my way to being one of them.

Dom had chilled out. Cairncross hadn't shifted in any sort of way, and I knew well enough that it was on me in my state of convergence to light the way. I did wonder—would restaurants like Ty's, or entertainment, art, music and sports still exist? Would we laugh and love just the same… how could we not? The notion of enjoyment suddenly consumed me to no end and for some reason I had a quesadilla on my mind. The urge to eat was so severe that, until I satisfied the potent longing for warm gooey queso, I could not do anything else—at all.

# 23

THE POWER OF now pulsed through my veins, electrifying my taste buds. I devoured those first bites, each one intensifying my hunger until nothing else existed. Was this a side effect of the Crystal Cloud?

"Is this seat taken?"

"Reba!!!"

I leapt from my chair and wrapped my arms around my long-lost friend. He chuckled, hugging me back with the lethargy of a sloth, while I buzzed like live wire.

"Where have you *been*?!" I squeezed his arms, unable to stop touching him, needing to believe he was real.

"Chica, I missed you, too, but you know I bruise easily."

I laughed and fell back into my seat for another cheesy chomp.

"I've been with you, though," he said, a glimmer in his sunken eyes. "I know you felt it."

I blinked, grounding myself to the sight of him. "But this —flesh and blood. Where I can *see* you."

"Here I am."

I squeezed him again. "I don't understand. Why were you gone so long?"

"Gone so long is a long story."

His eyes met mine, and suddenly, I got it.

"Want to order something?" I asked, my voice softening.

He shook his head. "My appetite's a mess. But you enjoy that quesadilla for both of us."

"Please tell me you're here to stay."

He looked thinner, haunted. His eyes were rimmed with exhaustion, hair hanging in limp strands, cheeks sunken and pale. Sadness radiated from him, and I wished I could erase it—but I knew better.

"Thanks for meeting me here," he whispered.

And it all made sense. My undying urge to be here hadn't just been hunger. It had been something *more*.

"This isn't just us hanging out, is it?" I asked, though I already knew.

"One day, it will be," he said, a strained smile stretching his face. "I know it."

"But?"

"Campbella..." His eyes welled up, the tears held prisoner. "I need you to be prepared. I couldn't let you go on without knowing."

A chill spread through me. "You're freaking me out, dude."

"What you're doing—it makes sense. Of course, it does. But someone is going to lose their life."

"Whoa, what?!"

"I'm sorry. I'm not trying to shock you."

"Who?!"

"It's not clear. Just… be careful."

"'Be careful.' That's all anyone says to me anymore."

"I want you to be ready for what's coming."

"Reba! Who's in danger?"

My mind spun, faces flipping like dominoes—Mom, Dad, Dom, Ellen. The Crystal Cloud didn't offer any clarity either.

"Please, Reba, think harder. Who? Why? I need to know."

He wiped his eyes, his voice thin. "It's not clear. I just know that on this path, someone will… die."

"That doesn't make sense. If you know that, you should know how to stop it."

"You have to keep going. This will play out, and you'll be at the center."

"Seriously?! Why would you say this to me if I need to keep going?"

His face crumpled. "Campbella, my whole heart led me here. You *know* that."

"You say that, but your actions—"

"I can sense the tragedy coming. I want you to be ready."

"You're asking me to trust something vague and immeasurable."

"Then don't turn it into an equation. Ultimate truth can't be measured—it can only be felt from where you stand."

Halfway through the quesadilla, my stomach twisted, the rich cheese turning to lead as worry crept in. Then, as if a dam burst, a rush of understanding swept away the nausea.

Reba was here because I was causing a disruption. A disruption that could jeopardize the Mars migration for the Intuerians. In the Aboves, Intuerians were treated like monsters. But in Seneca, they had equality. Justice. Reba's allegiance was to that promise. He'd been torn between his ethics, his loyalty to his people, society as a whole, and our friendship—a bond deeper than any societal construct.

"I'm sorry," I whispered. "I shouldn't have gone on the defense."

"It's okay," he said, and for a moment, the sadness lifted.

# 24

Moving ahead with our media blitz planning, we prepared for our trip to Hollenbeck Media headquarters in the Aboves. Julian Hollenbeck, Ellen, Dom, Yoshi, Professor Shields, and I were all part of the team. The headquarters had been run by Hollenbeck's daughter, Teddy, since Hollenbeck himself supposedly *died.* Ellen had leveraged her CIA status in the Aboves to land a private meeting with Teddy. This was a move that could cost her the Senecan status she invested her whole life to earning, but the risk was for the betterment of humanity and so this was not a hard choice for her to make.

Our crew took a private flight from Ronald Reagan Washington National Airport to JFK in New York, where a flighter scooped us and swooped us through some gusty winds onto the rooftop of Hollenbeck Media in the heart of Manhattan. Julian Hollenbeck was in full disguise as a national security agent—a crisp uniform, mirrored sunglasses, and a stiff walk—

while the rest of us wore sleek, all-black professional attire. I'd never looked so official. I felt like S.O.I.L. Ick. 'You gotta do what you gotta do,' I told myself.

We were greeted by a woman who approached and only spoke to Ellen, then walked us through a seemingly secret hallway to a conference room with a view fifty floors over the city. They say this city never sleeps, which basically meant that I felt right at home. Through the floor-to-ceiling window I saw flighters and cars stacked on top of one another, zigzagging through the city grid below us. Looking out, I could see all the way to the Brooklyn Bridge, which looked like a tiny lego model of the real thing, under a never-ending sky the color of stone. For a second, I was taken back to that day when Dom and I kissed on the bridge after I brought his memory back to him.

Teddy was alone in the conference room, standing looking out the window. The unspoken tension lingered—Teddy knew nothing about Seneca or the fact that her father had been alive and thriving in a global underground society for years. I imagined, though, that maybe she held on to a speck of hope that he was somewhere out there, like I did with my dad. Well, if this wasn't a moment of truth, I didn't know what was.

Teddy turned around to face us as we walked in. Her breath was shallow, as she clenched and unclenched her fingers, the nervous energy spilling out through her restless hands. She fidgeted, putting them in her pocket then pulling them out. I could relate—of course she was freaked out. "FBI" was coming on strong and she had absolutely no idea what this meeting was about. It was eerily familiar to the time Ellen and company were in my room with my mom when I got home from school. I was on the other side now, wishing Teddy would know that we hadn't come to mess with her. I tried to make eye contact with her, but her eyes were all over the place.

Ellen walked forward and extended her hand, "Hi, Miss Hollenbeck, I'm Ellen Malone."

"Please call me Teddy."

"I want you to know, right away, that we come in complete peace. You've done nothing wrong. Your company has done nothing wrong. We are here to ask for your help."

Teddy let out a sigh. "Well that's a relief… of sorts. What can I do for you?"

"Teddy Bear," Julian Hollenbeck quietly said from the back of our group. He removed his sunglasses and stepped out so that he was only a few feet away from Teddy.

Teddy's face went blank. She turned as white as a bed sheet and froze. The room went dead silent. Hollenbeck took a step towards her and Teddy's eyes widened. Her knees began to buckle and she looked like she was about to drop. Dom lunged forward to stop her from crumbling to the ground.

"Don't touch me!"

"Sorry, I'm just trying to help," Dom said, pulling his

arms back and putting them up as if he was under arrest.

"What the hell is this?" Teddy looked around to everyone except her dad.

We all turned to Ellen, because she always seemed to have the right words to say.

"Why don't we all sit down," Ellen suggested.

"I don't need to sit. Is this some cruel joke?"

"Teddy Bear—"

"There's no way. You don't think I know how you people run these manipulative machines—"

Hollenbeck was the first to take a seat. "Can I start by saying that I am sorry?"

Teddy looked at him out of the corner of her eye. I could tell she was holding back tears and trying to breathe normally but at any moment she could break.

"The last thing I ever wanted was to leave you."

Teddy's eyes slimmed on her dad.

"You know how sick I was," Julian said quietly.

Teddy shook her head.

"Best doctors on the face of the planet," he continued, "and they gave me weeks to live. Do you remember?"

Teddy apprehensively nodded in agreement.

"There was only one way for me to survive."

"Teddy," Ellen said, "I need you to understand and acknowledge that the level of information that is about to be shared with you is in breach of a level of security that puts all of us at risk, and that includes you."

Teddy finally took that seat. She didn't have a choice. She had to catch her breath and her legs had lost all of their function.

"Just give me a second." Teddy inhaled deep through her nose. She closed her eyes and blew out her mouth before opening them again to make sure this was reality. "UN-believable."

"Take all the time you need," Hollenbeck said to her. He walked up next to her and took a knee on the ground by her seat. He put his hand on her arm and looked into her eyes. Her shoulders trembled, a choked sob escaped, and she shook her head as tears spilled down her cheeks.

"I know," he said. "Life is crazy, Teddy Bear."

They put their arms around each other, and, in witnessing their affection I was pulled back into the vortex of timelessness. Teddy's confusion was met with love and it was like a limitless truth had magically rolled in to take all her pain away.

"I couldn't be more proud of what you've done here."

I felt a unity with this team deeper than anything I'd known before, a bond forged through shared risk and relentless hope. Within a half hour we were sitting close together around one end of the conference table, sifting through the top secret details of what brought every single one of us to this pinnacle of hope. The intention to release Doromium to the world surged through me like the blue veins pulsing beneath the South American wilderness—the same veins that led me to my dad, hidden away by the secrecy of The Seneca Society.

"Repairers and Departers alike have painted this as political warfare, getting everyone so engrossed in battle, that we all lost who we were and became only pawns in the struggle for power—you see, they've even separated us from our own families," Hollenbeck said to me.

"They took my dad away from me, too. But I found him," I said to Teddy. In that moment, the betrayal cut deep, the hollow ache of loss carved by Seneca's secrecy filled every part of me. Teddy gave me a nod, and I could feel the ties from our misfortunate experience of losing our dads. There was connection between the two of us.

Teddy looked to her dad. "I should have known. Here I am feeling awfully fulfilled with coverage on exploration, meanwhile all of this was happening right under our watch."

"Make no mistake, Miss Hollenbeck," Shields affirmed, "you have singlehandedly led a media empire through an era of madness and have done it with integrity and grace."

Ellen agreed. "Nobody in the Aboves who wasn't directly involved could have seen this coming."

Shields then added, "This agenda was contrived in

secrecy and covered up by two competing but mutually beneficial entities with incalculable resources. One in control of the software—cloud consciousness and flex—the other with the hardware—power plants, Martian robots, and so on. They're both pulling strings to leverage mankind, and *Doromium*, as an asset, starting with the intergalactic establishment of the highly secretive Seneca Society."

"You know what I still don't get though? If Flex Technology funded Seneca, why would they have S.E.R.C. scholars working on intergalactic communication speed if they didn't want to depart?" I asked.

Yoshi looked like a deer in headlights. I mean, this guy's mind was totally blown. This was literally all news to him. Every piece of it. He didn't say a word. It made sense that Teddy was confused, but Yoshi should have been somewhat up to speed at this point.

Shields answered, "The reality is, the Earth's resources are expendable. Even though eventually the sun will swallow Earth, at the rate we're consuming, we will swallow it far sooner. Migration is inevitable. Leaving for Mars is not preferred to staying here, but there needs to be a backup plan. The two sides need each other to lay the pipe."

Teddy nodded, sucking in her lips. "I know this part all too well. The fueling of a fear-driven narrative and creating existential anxiety. They scream and shout about the media, but the reality is the media is the medium, not the creator of the message."

Teddy had a flexer on her wrist that she used to turn up the volume on one of the monitors that encircled us in the room. It was coverage of the melting glaciers and flooding in the Pacific Northwest.

"Now you have information to release in the medium, because the truth is this is what our media was always about—giving truth and knowledge to the people. I am going to stay here with you and ensure that happens."

My eyes scanned across to a monitor that played footage of what looked like the barren wasteland version of Los Angeles. Burning hills, empty freeways cloaked in smoke that made the smog of my childhood look whimsical. I worried about Culver City, and my friends there who had no idea why this was happening, or that it could be prevented, even fixed. "Excuse me, Teddy, my flexer isn't networked to the Aboves. Is there one here I can make a flex on?"

"Try the next room over," she suggested, and nodded to one of her assistants to take me.

Ellen looked at her flexer. "You know what, Doro, we don't really have the time—"

"This will only take me two minutes. I promise. It's important."

I dipped out into the hallway before any further dialogue

had the chance to stop me. The assistant pointed me into a parallel conference room. I saw a flex center on the table and connected my network to it. I pulled Julie's flex contact from my Veil and set the outgoing caller as a nickname: "Killer's mom."

Julie answered. "Hello?" she said curiously.

"Thank god you answered."

"Doro?"

"Is anyone around you right now?"

"I can't believe you are calling me—"

"I know— listen—"

Then her tone changed. Her voice deepened. "You just leave and then call me out of the blue? How could you just bail? Never call or even send a message? Nothing!"

"Julie, I couldn't—I swear I would have—"

Julie's voice dripped with sarcasm. "This school must be something else." I could hear the hurt buried beneath her anger, the same hurt I'd felt when my dad vanished into Seneca's shadows.

"It's not a school, it's—Julie, I promise this will all make sense. I have so much to explain, and I will. I'm working on it. But please, just try to be happy that we get to connect for a minute right now."

"Happy?! You bailed, Doro! I was with you the whole time after your dad disappeared. You know what it's like when someone you love disappears."

"Of course I do—"

"Well imagine if your best friend is suddenly gone."

"Julie, please—"

Ellen came in and cupped my shoulder. I yanked it back involuntarily. "Doro, this is urgent—we have to get back."

"I love you, Julie. You're one of the most important people in my life, of all time! I'll come back. I promise. But I just need you to know one thing—when you see the news that's about to come out, I want you to believe it. I want you to know that it is all true."

Ellen tried to take the flexer from me—

"Ellen, wait!"

Julie's voice trembled on the other side of the line. "I hope you're happy in Virginia, or wherever it is that you moved to."

Before I had the chance to say another word, Ellen got the flexer away from me and disconnected it.

"Doro, you're out of control!"

"Don't you understand?"

"Of course I do! But do you understand that you are compromising us right now?! You have to be patient! She will be there, but not if you make amateur moves and mistakes like this. Get your emotions in check. Take some deep breaths and get your head back in the game."

My entire body trembled, grief and frustration tightening

my throat. Losing my dad to Seneca's secrecy was a scar I still carried, and now that same relentless secrecy was severing my connection with Julie, again. I saw double and couldn't stop the imagery of Kenneth Hahn Park going up in flames. That place was a sanctuary for me, my dad, my mom, my friends. Those were the last traces of green in my city.

Ellen and I hurried back into the conference room. When we walked in, our group was watching a report on a solar storm that was suddenly hitting the east coast.

"This isn't good," Teddy said.

"This too shall pass," Hollenbeck replied to her. "It always does." His calming voice extinguished some of my flames, but my heart still ached. Kenneth Hahn Park burning was a living nightmare. One that I needed to wake up from, and there was only one way to do it. Release Doromium into the atmosphere immediately and begin the repair.

"Our flighter is here," Ellen said.

# 25

THE SKIES WERE empty on our quiet ride to Great Falls, save for the occasional flash of headlights as the number of people outdoors had reduced exponentially since I'd gone to Seneca. I leaned against the window, my eyes drifting across the landscape devoid of human energy. Beside me, Dom shifted with unease.

We eventually made it to the girls' ambassador house where Jennifer stayed. The house stood secluded, bathed in shadows from trees that engulfed it. The darkness here played to our rising anxiety as we landed on the perimeter, outside of any possible surveillance. I had built shields on our flexers so we wouldn't be detected.

Ellen was the first to step out of our flighter with a decisive stance, her eyes scanning the property. I followed, my heart pounding. I remembered the nights I spent in one of the guest rooms here, surrounded by modern luxury yet feeling the unspoken history that seemed to seep from the walls, with expectations and power struggles that defined the Wallingsford family and their inner circles.

Jennifer met us at the door, her posture stiff per the usual. She hadn't changed much since I last saw her. Her eyes narrowed slightly as she took in the group, lingering on Ellen before shifting back to me.

"I hope you have a very good reason for coming here," Jennifer said, her voice edged with caution. She crossed her arms, her stance guarded.

I stepped forward. "I know this visit may come as a surprise, but I am sure you can imagine I wouldn't be here like this, with this group, if I didn't need to be."

"Alright," Jennifer said, prompting an immediate explanation with her tone.

"FlexCorp and S.O.I.L. are making moves that will put everyone at risk– including your family. We need your help." My voice cracked a bit as it was laced with desperation.

Jennifer remained silent, her eyes assessing me, then moving to the rest of the team—Dom, standing close behind me; Ellen, her expression unreadable; Professor Shields, who gave Jennifer a small, almost pleading nod. "What is it that you want from me?" Jennifer asked.

"This isn't just about us," I said, softening. "It's about everyone in Seneca."

Ellen addressed Jennifer directly now. "We need a way

back in, and you're the only one who can help us do that—undetectable."

Jennifer gave Ellen an affirmative nod. Then she sighed, her concentration shifting. She turned her head, looking past me into the darkness. "Dorothy, you know I trust in your intentions, and Ellen you've been a friend of my family's since I was little, but you all have no idea what you're asking of me," she said, her voice barely above a whisper. "If I help you, it's not just my life on the line. There are people I care about… people who could get hurt."

I stepped closer, my voice lowering. "If we don't do something right now, there won't be anything left to protect. I know that you understand why I am doing this."

Jennifer's eyes met mine, and something unspoken passed between us—a shared understanding of the risks and the impossible choices we all had to make. Since the moment we met there was a trust between us and we had done nothing but prove that we were worthy of it.

Finally, Jennifer exhaled, her shoulders relaxing slightly. "Alright," she said, her voice resigned. "But we do this my way. Wait here while I get my things."

She seemed to pause for a moment just before turning to walk inside. She looked as if she was debating something to herself, then disappeared inside. For what felt like a long few minutes, we waited—wondering if she was about to sell us out.

Eventually she reappeared, signaling for us to follow her. "We have to get to my family's estate on the other side of the woods. I can get us past the grounds' security easily enough, but we still need a solid distraction to get us into the main family home. There's a basement entrance there that leads into a bunker and Seneca's maintenance tunnels. It's the safest way, but getting in will be tricky," she stated with a shakiness in her voice.

"Doro, you need to buy us some time," she continued, looking at me. "I need you to prepare a flex to my brother. Make it look like it's from my father. Tell him that the flighter broke down in D.C., and he needs to get there immediately. I know you know how to do that sort of thing."

I nodded. "Easy." I stepped forward and accessed my flex implant. The familiar, almost undetectable hum of the connection settled into my mind as I accessed the secure network of flexers in the Aboves.

"If G.W. thinks our father is stranded in D.C., it'll keep him occupied long enough for us to do what we need to do," Jennifer explained.

I focused, using my flex implant to forge the message, embedding all the necessary encryption and verification markers to make it look authentic. After getting it prepped, I looked up. "Alright."

Jennifer gave a small nod of approval. "When we get to

my father's property, we'll send the flex. That'll give us the assurance we have a small window of time.

"Sounds like a plan," I said, looking to the others for agreement, which they did.

"Let's get going."

We left the ambassadors' house under the cover of darkness, moving swiftly through the dense surrounding woods towards the main estate a few miles away. The journey was long and nerve-wracking, the grove enveloping us as we moved swiftly through a narrow game path. The moonlight slivered through the canopy above us.

Every rustle of leaves or snap of a branch had us on edge, making us freeze for a heartbeat before pressing on. The woods seemed endless, the cold air biting as we made our way through in silence, each of us peering through branches in different directions hoping no one else was peering back.

After what felt like an eternity, the dark silhouette of the main Wallingsford estate finally came into view. Its grand structure loomed over us. Jennifer paused, crouching down and gesturing for us to stay low as we approached, avoiding the motion sensors embedded discreetly along the property's edges.

When we approached the estate, the main house's silhouette was outlined by the starry night sky. The high-tech barriers were hidden, but I knew they were there—silent sentinels guarding the Wallingsford legacy.

"Alright," she whispered, her voice trembling. "We're close. Doro, it's time to send the flex."

I nodded, and made my move. Jennifer watched me closely, her expression a mix of concern and determination. After a moment, I looked up. "It's sent."

Jennifer gave a tight smile. "Good. That should ensure we don't have any surprises for now. Follow me."

She led us to the entrance of the main house. The Wallingsford mansion was a testament to wealth and history. The place felt imposing, and carried the weight of a place where secrets were kept behind closed doors, but now it carried a sense of danger, also.

It was the kind of place that spoke of generations of influence—a sprawling estate hidden behind tall gates, that held its power through manicured woods. The exterior had an old-world elegance, but the security... the security was unmistakably modern. I had never noticed it before, but I guess I never needed to. I thought about how blind I had been, never noticing the authoritarian surveillance and high-tech barriers woven seamlessly into the architecture around this place. Maybe it was because I wasn't looking since when I first came here I thought it was just for boarding school.

On the inside the interior was as grand as anyone would imagine—dark wood paneling, marble floors, and portraits of the Wallingsford lineage hanging in opulent frames, now a stark reminder of Senator Frank Wallingsford's influence and Jennifer's privileged, yet burdened, upbringing. I couldn't have imagined growing up like this. It was nothing like my life in L.A.

Jennifer led us through the hallway, her footsteps barely making a sound on the polished marble floor. We moved deeper inside the house, away from the main rooms, until she stopped in front of a door that seemed out of place—heavier, reinforced. She paused, her hand on an unmarked spot on the door, and turned to look at us.

"This is the way in," she said, her voice quiet. "It's not exactly official, but it'll get you where you need to go." The door opened after her hand rested there for thirty seconds, revealing a narrow staircase descending into darkness. The air was cooler here, carrying a faint scent of earth and dampness. Ellen stepped forward, peering down the staircase. "How far does it go?" she asked, her tone practical.

Jennifer glanced at Ellen, then back at me. "It leads to a bunker, and then another door that leads to a series of old maintenance tunnels. Seneca's infrastructure is as endless as the earth—there are parts of it even S.O.I.L. doesn't fully know about. You can use these to get close without being detected."

I nodded, a sense of both dread and determination settling in. "How risky is it?" I asked, needing to know what we were walking into.

Jennifer hesitated. "It's risky," she admitted. "There are patrols, sensors… but if you're careful, you can avoid them. I've mapped out the route as best as I could based on my family's own evacuation plans. Here. Take this. Once you're in, move quickly."

Dom stepped closer, "We're ready for this, Doro."

Jennifer looked at each of us in turn, her expression a mix of resolve and reluctance. "Alright," she said, "good luck."

"Jennifer. Thank you," I said.

"Thank *you*, Dorothy. See you on the other side."

We started our way in but Shields held back.

"Professor?" I questioned.

"Someone from our crew needs to hang back and be our eyes, ears, and voice up here."

He was right.

Ellen extended her hand to Professor Shields, "You've been nothing short of loyal to Seneca and all of us for as long as I've known you."

I sensed a spark between them—a moment I wished they could explore beyond right now.

Shields hugged her. She closed her eyes but then pulled away and didn't look back. None of us did. We knew this was not a time to let emotions into the mix. As we left Jennifer and headed inside, the darkness seemed to close in around us, the air dropping a few degrees with each step. We illuminated our surroundings with our flexers. My heart pounded in my chest. The stairs led us into a narrow tunnel, barely wide enough for two people to walk side-by-side. Ellen took the lead next to me, her eyes scanning for any signs of trouble. Yoshi and Dom brought up the rear. Yoshi's usually nonchalant demeanor was replaced by a focused intensity, as he kept watch.

I could tell Dom stayed in the back to have an eye on us all. As we navigated the uneven ground, my eyes adjusted to the dim light. Ellen paused at a junction, her wrist-light casting a faint glow on the walls. "The map says this way," she said, pointing to the right. But she suddenly stopped.

"Ellen, we all good?" I asked.

"I hope we don't need to use this, but I want you to have it. Just in case."

She pulled out a sleek device, with a few attachments visible in the limited light. My fingers brushed the surface of the weapon and I took it carefully into my hand.

"This is a Sonic Disruptor," she explained. "It emits sonic waves that disarm enemies by disrupting their neural pathways." She paused, looking at the device. "Do you think you could handle it, if you needed to?"

"If it came down to it, I think so. I've never used one before, but I know what it can do."

As we continued, I was attuned to the soft scuffle of our footsteps and the occasional disembodied sniff from someone behind me. My senses were on high alert, every shadow and sound making my heart race.

Ellen stopped abruptly, holding up a hand. “Wait,” she whispered. We all froze. She gestured for us to move back, her eyes narrowing as she listened. In the distance, I could hear the faint hum of something mechanical—a patrol drone.

“Everyone, stay still,” Ellen whispered and moved closer to the wall.

Dom squeezed past Yoshi to be next to me. I felt the warmth of his body protecting me. I held my breath. The hum grew louder, then slowly began to fade as the drone moved away, oblivious to our presence. Ellen waited a few more moments before nodding, signaling us to continue.

# 26

THE TUNNEL YAWNED before us—a secret passage carved into the earth's crust. The air clung cool and damp against my skin. Shadows curled along the walls.

Ellen led, her wrist-light a slender beam through the dark. Behind her, I followed, the significance of our mission an unflinching weight nestled between my shoulders. Dom's footsteps had a familiar rhythm. It was oddly comforting that I could recognize his footsteps so clearly now.

The tunnel wound on, narrowing like a secret held too tightly. The walls closed in, urging us to move single file. Time felt suspended here, ancient moments pressing in. My breathing slowed, each inhale thin and careful, laced with anticipation. Every sound became a ripple—the delicate drip of moisture from cracks in the earth.

My flex implant was busy. Data streams flowed beneath my consciousness like strands of silk. Seneca's network glowed with life, a pattern of protocols, movements, and encrypted intel. S.O.I.L.'s patrol patterns were a grim echo of those tense days at Claytor Lake when Dom and I worked on The Brooklyn Project to dismantle the nanobots, before I went to search for my dad. Little did we know our work would be far from over.

I tuned in, letting meaning blossom from the chaos, fragments crystallizing into clear shapes. "Two guards," I murmured, the images blooming behind my eyes. "They'll move in five minutes."

"How do you know?" Dom asked.

I met his gaze, the answer too intricate to explain. My flex and the Crystal Cloud had merged, the developing connection now an intimate part of me. Severing it would be like losing a piece of my own rapidly accelerating mind.

Ellen's voice, calm and certain, broke through the dark. "We time it perfectly."

Dom's eyes reflected the thin beam of light, wide and cautious. He had seen this before—how the data coursed through me, giving me an edge, a brush against the unknown. But tonight, that unknown felt more delicate, like we were tiptoeing on the edge of something so immense but it could explode at any moment.

A rusted metal door loomed ahead—patched and worn, streaked with the colors of age. But beneath its decay, modern veins of security tech pulsed silently. My fingers danced across the control panel, tracing its paths like a familiar arrangement. A soft chime sang as the lock yielded. "This leads to the lower levels," I whispered, easing the door open.

We stepped through into a mechanical cavern. Conduits lined the walls like veins, and the air felt alive with a current of information processing. It was as if we were inside a living system. The reality was, we were. The warmth here softened the chill, heat rising from some unseen, industrious heart.

"Stay close," Ellen said. Her firmness felt protective and gave me even more confidence. We moved as one. My flex implant kept coming with the data—patrol paths, intersecting feeds, fragments of encrypted chatter. The network pulsed faster, each piece a clue leading us deeper.

"Wait," I said. A clap of a warning—patrol, northwest corridor. "Don't move."

Ellen's jaw tightened. "Alternate route?"

I shook my head. "Not unless you want to lose hours."

"Then we wait," she said with certainty.

Dom's hand brushed mine, his touch a trace of comfort. I closed my eyes, sinking into the rhythm of the network's pulse. The drone's movements were smooth, a graceful predictability. I counted down, each second a measured breath. The clock ticked in slow motion.

"Now," I murmured. "Two minutes."

We slipped forward, shadows blending into shadows.

Pipes curled along the walls like quiet custodians, their flow of energy guiding us along. Each step deepened the ache in my chest—these secrets were getting too heavy to hold for long. Seneca's unseen machinery surrounded us. I was choosing to become integrated in this system instead of fearing it, but it was hard not to feel swallowed by it.

The control systems were near. My flex implant sparked, a rush of data opening to the sun like flowers behind my eyes. Security wrapped around this place, layers of code and steel woven together—a shield protecting truths.

I pressed my hand against the terminal, the cool metal a sharp bite against my palm. My implant synced, and data flowed gently in, defenses stirring at the edge of my thoughts. Each layer was a lock, intricate and waiting. My focus sharpened, the world blurring away.

"You've got this," Dom said.

He saw the intensity of the process brewing behind my eyes.

I moved quickly, my fingers brushing the interface melodically. I heard music playing in my mind as code loosened, firewalls unfolded. The sweat cooled on my temple. Each second felt stretched, expectation hanging like mist.

Then—an alarm, sharp and sudden.

"We've been detected," Ellen said, her eyes bright. Fight or flight.

"Thirty seconds," I breathed, my fingers trembling.

"You don't have thirty," Ellen said firmly.

Dom's hand on the small of my back steadied me. I pushed harder. The defenses faltered, a fragile glow appeared. I struck—the connection shattered.

The alarms faded, the silence settling like a held breath.

"I'm in."

Dom's hand closed around mine, pulling me forward: Run. Footsteps echoed—agents closing in, a ripple through the broken calm.

"They know," I murmured. "Sector B-13."

"Then they're setting traps," Ellen said.

"Let them," I replied.

The corridor widened, opening into a chamber of pale blue light. At its center, an illuminated monolith—a graceful cylinder, veins of light flowing beneath its surface. The air thrummed, alive with energy. I'd been pulled here.

"An energy source for the Crystal Cloud," I breathed, wonder in my voice.

Ellen's eyes searched the room. "Doro, can you sever it?"

I stepped forward, nerves fluttering. The core pulsed, sensing me. My flex implant glowed with data flowing in like a warm tide.

I touched the interface. The connection flared, the

network an expansive web. I felt probed, tested. But I dove deeper, letting my intention steer me through the noise. Patterns appeared, as did weaknesses hidden beneath. The cloud resisted, firm yet yielding.

My mind felt strained and I grasped my temples.

"We've got you," Dom assured me, but I saw him slipping. I felt him slipping. Something of an undertone inside the Crystal Cloud was taking over Dom's body from the inside.

I reached further with uncanny precision. The nexus glowed, fragile and open. I was on the verge of severing the link. The core dimmed, the light fading to stillness.

Dom's eyes met mine, holding a wary kind of trust. He understood it all now—the way the data flowed through me, making me just a step ahead. We needed that edge. The collective intelligence of the Crystal Cloud.

A jagged breath escaped him. "We need you to stay connected."

I hated the truth in his voice. It scraped against every instinct to protect him. But he was right. I had to be in the Crystal Cloud to understand the Crystal Cloud. It was equally my ally and my enemy.

"I know," I said, the words bitter on my tongue.

His jaw tightened, a reluctant acceptance mirrored in my own chest. We were both compromised now, and Dom's life hung on the thinness of our options.

"Just don't lose yourself in it," he pleaded.

# 27

DOM COLLAPSED AGAINST the wall. His skin was slick and pale. The tremors in his limbs told me the nanobots were raging—like fire spreading through his blood, unstoppable. I knelt beside him, my hands shaking as they cradled his face. “Dom, tell me what you want me to do.”

His eyes fluttered open, clouded with pain. "It’s... my own design," he rasped. "I built this. I did this. And now I'm going to pay."

His words struck deep. He had created this—this thing—now it was destroying him. The realization twisted inside me like a knife. The same technology that coursed through Dom’s veins was perfected in the sterile halls of the Claytor Lake medical hub. What they built to heal could just as easily destroy.

“I never meant for this,” he choked, his voice breaking.

I pressed my forehead against his, the chill of his skin sharp against me.

"It's not your fault. They did this. They made it into something it was never meant to be so they would control us."

My words felt empty, drifting in the space between us.

"We have to sever the connection. Now! Yoshi! These bots are no different than the Martian bots. There's a control bot, deep in their network. It's manipulating the swarm. We need to decode its command language to break the link but stay in the Cloud."

Yoshi stepped forward, his eyes glowing with determination, the maze of data hitting his flexer from mine.

"I'm recognizing their patterns," he said. "They speak in pulses. Like a dance. Rhythm and counter-rhythm."

"Then let's dance," Ellen said, her eyes on Dom with worry. I could tell that Dom felt Ellen's support.

Yoshi's fingers flew over his holographic console, the air around us alive with code. It writhed like a living thing, coiling and stretching, threads of logic binding it together and encircling us with glowing circuits. Yoshi's focus was a storm. Eyes darting, brow furrowed, hunting for the right sequence.

"Here," he said, his voice tight. "This pattern controls the swarm. If we disrupt it—introduce a counter-pattern—we might be able to break the link."

Dom's body arched, a gasp tearing through him. The swarm surged, a wave crashing against him.

"Do it," I urged. "He won't last much longer, Yoshi,

please!"

Yoshi nodded, sweat dotting his forehead, his fingers dancing across the console. The world around us shrank to the beat of his robot programming code.

"Do not mess this up. Do not mess this up," Yoshi muttered to himself. When the system finally unlocked, he exhaled hard, his hands still trembling. His grin was faint, edged with disbelief.

"I am in," he said, almost like he was reassuring himself before he made a final determined strike—Yoshi whispered, "Sever."

Dom convulsed once, then went still.

Ellen placed a hand on my shoulder, her own body taut with confusion and grief. But I felt the weight lifting—*he's not gone*, I thought.

His eyes opened—soft, pained, but alive. "You did it," he whispered, his voice cracked and weak.

Yoshi's smile was faint, but it carried a relief that barely had time to settle. My flex implant pulsed—a cold, electric warning. Data flashed, jagged and urgent. "They're regrouping," I said, voice low. "The Crystal Cloud is recalibrating to reconnect the nanobot line. It will be near impossible to fend off its capabilities."

Yoshi's fingers were still moving over his console, scanning the data. "The bots in Dom are dormant, but this does not end here. The bots might recalibrate themselves… or the system will evolve."

"It is evolving," I added.

Suddenly two S.O.I.L. agents ran in on a sneak attack, fast and precise, their weapons raised. Ellen's hand shot to her sonic disruptor, lifting it in a swift, practiced motion. But I felt a jolt through the air. My instinct screamed. "Don't shoot!"

Ellen froze, her finger hovering above the trigger. The agents paused too, assessing. The seconds stretched out and everything moved in slow motion, even sound. Then, like a storm breaking in the middle of a still night, a hooded figure moved in. His body was a blur of motion—fast and fluid. He was on the first S.O.I.L. agent in an instant, twisting his wrist so violently the weapon clattered to the floor. The second agent reacted, lunging toward him, but the hooded figure was already sidestepping, and swiftly swept the agent's legs out from under him. The agent slammed into the ground, breath knocked out. The hooded figure was on him in a split second, his arm locking around the agent's neck, his movements precise—like the calm at the center of chaos. No hesitation. No words. Just the crack of bones and the weight of the fight ending in seconds.

It was done. The agents were left crumpled on the floor, incapacitated, and silent.

My dad came out of the shadow from the edge of the room, watching the aftermath unfold. His presence filled the space without a word, his eyes steady, sharp, and calm.

"Dad!" I was shocked!

The stealth figure pulled his hood back. "Jadel!" My voice cracked—caught between disbelief and overwhelming relief. He nodded and stepped back, his focus never leaving my dad.

The two of them shared a brief moment of recognition, but it was my dad's eyes that met mine next. In that moment, I saw everything—the weight of years spent searching, the toll of the journey that had brought him here. I swallowed hard. "How did you find me?"

"Jadel found you," he replied, his voice low but certain. "I came to make sure you were safe. And to ensure that Doromium—*your* birthright—will be freed to the world."

"I can gather the allies," I murmured, almost to myself, as the realization came in and the pieces fell into place. And then, out loud, I declared, "The allies are waiting for our signal!"

I glanced at Dom. His breath was slow, but he was still alive, still with us.

Ellen stepped forward, addressing my dad directly. "Johnny Campbell. Do you remember me?

"Of course I do," he said, extending his hand to Ellen.

"Thank you—for everything. You tell us what you need from us right now," Ellen said with more excitement in her voice than I'd ever heard.

"I should thank you for looking out for my little girl."

The clarity of the moment settled over me, and before my dad had a chance to answer Ellen, I spoke, "We need to get to B3 before S.O.I.L. assesses and shuts down the media."

Ellen nodded and zeroed in on me. "Remember why we're here, Doro. It's not just about breaking in—"

I finished her sentence. "It's about breaking free."

# 28

ALMOST AS INSTANTANEOUSLY as I had the idea, the plan arrived and I became a node in a vast web that stretched across the planet. It was alive and waiting for me to arrive. I closed my eyes and let myself sink in deeper. I felt the illumination in every piece of me.

*Threads of connection.*

From every stolen signal, every hijacked frequency, I could feel the reach of our message extending outward like ripples in a dark sea. My consciousness, now woven into this living network, brushed against minds waking to the call of revolution.

It was more than data. It was life.

Reaching.

Connecting.

Becoming.

I breathed in, and the world breathed back through the

very technology that had been outlawed and then taken as a tool in the arsenal for the corrupt.

Our message flexed out in a current to the like-minded:

*The time has come for us to take back the tools of oppression. Help us reshape the world.*

The streams of information I'd been holding onto burst through encrypted pathways and dark-web channels, uncoiling like a vine into every corner of the planet.

One-by-one they answered.

First, a spark—a pinprick of light. Then a cascade.

They rose: scientists, thinkers, dreamers, fighters.

Each response was a note in the symphony, a pulse of energy that strengthened the web, binding us all together.

Some voices were elevated to represent whole groups.

Dr. Reva Chandra's voice crackled to life, clear and unwavering despite the distance.

*I've been waiting for this moment.*

She spoke, connected to us like a steel pipeline of promise.

*I know the redundancies in their network. I can help bring them down.*

Her voice was woven with the rest into the network, strengthening the web. A bridge forged.

Another face came into view—a man with lines carved deep by wind and sun. Elias Tuwima, a man in his eighties whose voice carried the knowledge of mountains and rivers.

*The poison runs deep. But the roots of the world are older. We'll help you pull it out.*

His words wrapped around me, grounding the fight in something before human life, something unbreakable. A tether to the earth itself. And more followed.

Scientists, their hands stained by past compromises, now reaching to cleanse what they had unwittingly built. Activists, their voices hoarse from years of shouting into voids now filled with possibility. Indigenous leaders, protectors of the land and its truths, ready to reclaim what had been stolen. I felt them all. My consciousness stretched out, brushing theirs, merging intention and resolve. We became a network of defiance, a tapestry of shared purpose.

A global exhale.

We were no longer fragments. We were a whole.

On the inhale a bead of light floated around me, followed by many more. I became enveloped in the Intuerian Agenda. A knowingness that spanned across time and space to tell me that we were all exactly where we needed to be, right here, right now. To know that it would get dark before we saw the light. And to stay strong. I knew Reba was in this message. I knew it was true and I knew exactly what we needed to do.

Jadel's voice, clear and fierce, broke through the barrier I was swimming beneath.

"We need our network to reach the indigenous in Peru. They can overpower the security measures once you sever the tech, and release Doromium. We give them the power to rise."

Jadel understood the power of the ancients. He believed. He saw the web for what it was: not chaos, but possibility.

"Are you sure about the release?" Ellen's voice was taut, the edge of caution sharpening it. "What if we lose control? What if it's too much, too soon?" My connection thrummed as I echoed Ellen's fear and it wove its way through the web, a shadow pushing its way between the lights. But even shadows are part of the whole.

I spoke, feeling my voice travel through the network. "We don't control it. We guide it. We give the world the choice FlexCorp and SGE tried to steal. The web is strong enough to hold both chaos and hope."

Jadel nodded. "We trust the will of the people. It is all we *can* trust."

I felt a wave of agreement roll through the network—a consensus made between thousands of minds, a thousand breaths… it would soon become a million.

More.

Amid the surge of voices joining the revolution, a new signal pulsed in the network. It was cautious at first, like someone stepping out of shadows they'd hidden in for too long. Then a familiar voice resonated through the flex.

*This is Dr. Ashvind Kulkarni.*

A chill ran through me. The name felt like a dark stain on my mind. He was one of the doctors who had perfected and administered Cogniz-X—the drug used to erase memories of the Seneca Society for those who chose to return to the Aboves, transforming resistance into compliance. He was also the one who injected me with Vigilogstimine to restore my bodily functions after S.O.I.L. left me paralyzed.

The network hushed, a collective intake of breath, waiting for his justification. His defense. His excuses. But none came.

His message was trembling slightly, carrying the weight of regret.

*I've been complicit in stealing people's pasts, their identities. I thought I was serving security, stability. But I see now—I was serving control. I was serving fear.*

A beat of silence. Then his message strengthened.

*I can't undo what I've taken from people. But I can help give it back.*

A data packet unfolded. My flex glowed with the information—sequences for memory-recovery protocols, tools to counteract the injections and restore what had been lost.

*I'm sharing everything I know. This protocol will help people reclaim their memories. Their truth. No more secrets. No more stolen identities. Use it to heal those I've harmed.*

The network reverberated with realization. Medics, techs, and resistance leaders seized the data, already planning its deployment. I could feel it—the first sparks of restoration, the light of lost stories ready to be returned.

I sent a pulse of acknowledgment through the network. Not forgiveness. But acceptance of his choice to repair, to rebuild. He couldn't change the past. But he could help us reclaim it.

Ellen's jaw unclenched. She nodded and her resolve, too, folded into the web. "I knew it from the moment I met you in your home, Doro. Your bright mind would take us somewhere."

"You believed in me when nobody else did."

"And now this is working because you believe, too."

This was it. The moment before our entire existence shifted. I could feel the connective fibers drawn together with readiness, tingling with the collective mind of humanity.

A tremor in the web pulled my focus back. A frayed strand, a disturbance reverberating with an icy punch to the gut.

I turned, and the brilliance of the network faded.

Dom was slumped against the console, his skin almost translucent. His breath came in shallow gasps, his eyes fluttering as if caught between wakefulness and some deeper, darker place.

The cold reality struck like ice water.

The web vibrated with life, but Dom's thread was

unraveling, and in an instant, I was pulled back to *here and now.* I was at his side, my fingers brushing his forehead. He was burning and freezing all at once, the heat of the swarm battling the cold depths of betrayal in his blood. His voice was a breath barely hanging on, trembling against the noise of the network, "It's… spreading."

I clenched my jaw, forcing back the tears that threatened to blur my vision. I couldn't lose him—not now. Not when we were so close.

The others gathered around my dad, Ellen, Jadel, Yoshi, the brilliance of our plan now shadowed by Dom's pain. The web was strong, but this strand—this single strand—felt like it was about to snap.

"We have to stop it," I pleaded. "We can't let it spread any further."

My dad's hand landed on my shoulder. "Find the source, Doro. Cut the strings they're using to control him."

I nodded, my mind torn between the infinite reach of the network and the raw, aching reality of Dom's pain. The web held millions of lives, but this life—his life—was slipping through my fingers like sand.

Just then, a message cut through the web, a new beam of light. I felt a surge of recognition and hope. Anika's voice came through, excited and filled with unwavering belief.

*I knew you'd come through! Josie and I have been*

*preparing for this and we will support from The Aboves!*

As her words spread across the network, I felt the power of her message ripple through me. It was a force I could almost grab with my hands. It was like a jolt of clarity. But it didn't stop with me—it shot straight into Dom. I could feel him, just for a moment, taking in the warmth of her presence. Anika had been an old friend of his family, a trusted ally. Her message, her belief, seeped into the web like a lifeline for Dom.

Ellen's eyes locked on mine. "We don't stop the plan, Doro. We can't. We keep going. We do it for him."

I swallowed hard, feeling a weight in my chest. The web pulsed, a living presence, waiting for the final spark. Dom's hand wrapped weakly around mine. His eyes, clouded but determined, met mine.

"I'm with you," he whispered. "Stay connected and give it your all."

I squeezed his hand, pouring my strength into that fragile strand of silk. "Always."

I turned back into the web, back to the world waiting for us to strike the match. Suddenly, without even asking, it was as if the Crystal Cloud knew exactly what I needed. Encrypted S.O.I.L. maps of Seneca's entrance points flooded my mind, the digital grid unfurling in vivid detail. The map materialized as a holographic grand plan. Access points and locations aligned seamlessly in the air before me. The maintenance tunnels, hidden paths, and secure entryways illuminated. I followed the path with my finger, tracing it until I found it—the way in. The entrance was just ahead.

Without a word, the map flashed and expanded, presenting itself to the team. They saw it, too, understood it, and there was no hesitation. Each of us locked eyes with one another, a silent understanding passing between us… and we booked it!

# 29

THE CARRIER GLIDED forward, riding the sound waves. The absence of noise made the motion feel more eerie than normal. I tightened my grip on the controls. Through the plexiglass windshield, the Senecan hub blurred in streaks of white and gold. We were slicing through corridors of light and metal, on our way to make waves with B3 Media.

Jadel was in the front row, just behind me, his deep green eyes scanning all of our surroundings at all times. Ellen sat quietly next to him. I saw them in the reflection in the window in front of me. Ellen had almost shot Jadel. A second more, and everything would've changed.

"Close call," Ellen muttered in her signature monotone, but something heavier sat beneath her voice. She didn't think I could hear her, but the Cloud's effect had sharpened my hearing to something almost wolf-like.

Jadel exhaled deeply. "I have had closer ones. But… not

many." His arms were crossed tight, his shoulders rigid.

Ellen's fingers tapped a rhythm on her thigh that only she understood. "Berlin," she said, her voice stripped of armor. "I didn't think I'd make it out."

Jadel's gaze slid to her, dark and knowing. "For me… Cairo. Different city. Same poison."

She nodded slowly. "You stop trusting everything—the ground beneath your feet, the air you breathe, the people…"

"Yourself," Jadel added, his words slow, deliberate.

Ellen nodded, wishing that wasn't true, but accepting it.

Their interaction was mesmerizing to me. They'd just met but they were letting each other in more than they'd let most people *ever*, I imagined.

"They teach you, see enemy everywhere," Jadel said, hushed.

"I thought leaving would set me free," Ellen added. "But now it feels like all of that was just preparation for *this*."

Jadel tilted his head, considering her words. "Everything before… just training. For this?" He gestured faintly to the rest of us on the carrier. "This is the real fight."

Ellen's eyes softened. "Do you ever think we're just playing out someone else's endgame?"

Jadel's jaw tightened, then relaxed. "Not this time. This time, we hold the pieces and make the moves."

She turned to him. "What happens for you if we win?"

Jadel's eyes held hers, the hardness there giving way to something quieter. "Then we finally learn who we are… without the fight."

She drew in a breath, held it a moment. "That sounds terrifying."

"Possible." His shoulders eased, just a little. "But maybe… worth it?"

They weren't looking at each other, but they were seeing the same thing. The world as it could be. The world as they hoped to leave it.

My dad was a silent watchman on the back of the acoustic carrier. I could tell he was concerned for Dom. Even though they'd just met, I knew he saw my connection with Dom. I could sense that my dad felt responsible for everyone's pain.

Dom was slumped against the back panel of the acoustic carrier, his skin pale and clammy. His breaths were shallow, his eyes half-lidded, caught in a space between consciousness and fevered dreams. They'd broken him down, shredded his mind, and I had to keep him plugged in so that I could be in the grid and the Crystal Cloud… and that might destroy him.

*It might destroy both of us.*

Yoshi popped up from a cat nap. "Almost at the drop point?" he muttered, more to himself than anyone else. His voice was positive, but the strain in his eyes gave him away.

I took a massive breath and looked around to everyone,

landing back on Yoshi, my unexpected sidekick. "We're almost there, can you take the controls?"

As I got up and moved back to Dom, his eyes opened to a sliver, glassy and unfocused. He turned his head toward me, his voice a rough whisper. "Doro…"

I moved over to him, taking his icy hand in mine. His fingers trembled, but he squeezed back, his grip like a glitching code-link.

"I'm here," I whispered, my voice shaking.

His lips twitched, almost a smile, but his eyes darkened. "I don't know if I can hold it together this time."

A wave of fear crashed over me. My mind spun with worst-case scenarios: Dom's mind fracturing, his body crumpling, losing him to a place where I couldn't follow. But I shoved the thoughts down, locking them away.

"You don't have to," I said. "I've got you."

He let out a shaky breath, his forehead pressing against mine. His skin burned, a stark contrast to the cold seeping through his hands. The silence around us was deafening—a vacuum of sound and certainty.

*What if I'm wrong? What if I lose him?*

The carrier slowed, a barely perceptible shift in momentum. We were at the edge of B3. The Crytal Cloud's data lattice, the S.O.I.L. guards' encrypted defenses—they were all waiting for us, pillars in an intricate web only I could untangle.

I closed my eyes, feeling the sharp sting of tears I couldn't let fall. "Stay with me, Dom."

He pulled back enough to look at me, his eyes burning with a fragile, unyielding light. "I'll try."

Yoshi's quiet voice broke through the stillness. "We're here."

The carrier eased to a stop. The world outside was a gleaming media fortress. My pulse quickened as I knew S.O.I.L. was out there, invisible but deadly—an intricate network of security systems designed to detect, intercept, and obliterate any intruder. But they were built on logic. On patterns. On probabilities.

I wasn't bound by those rules.

I closed my eyes, reaching deep into that space beyond thought, beyond matter—where particles danced in entangled pairs, where distance and time unraveled. The quantum field shimmered behind my eyelids, a web of light and possibility.

*Everything is light. Everything is connected. Let the light guide you.*

The S.O.I.L. system flared to life in my mind, its pathways lighting up and attaching like mirrors to my neural circuits. Threat-assessment nodes, encryption loops, self-repairing firewalls—all predictable once you knew how to see them.

*Move before they sense you. Anticipate their logic. Be*

*the ghost in their machine.*

I exhaled slowly, and the S.O.I.L. system popped—a spike of awareness—but I was already ahead of it, weaving us through the gaps, dissolving like mist before it could focus.

Dom's hand gripped mine, his strength returning in that silent, desperate connection. We were in this together—two particles bound by something beyond the mind's comprehension.

Ellen was by my side. "Doro, are you ready?"

"Yes," I whispered.

This was the heart of it all—where news was shaped, narratives were controlled, and truths were buried under layers of polished lies. We were about to change that.

I looked at Dom. His eyes were clear now, the fever momentarily forgotten. He nodded, the hint of a smile tugging at his lips. "Let's make some noise."

Our carrier glided into the resting, kinetic atmosphere of B3 Media. The future was waiting, and we were ready to write it.

# 30

THE CARRIER ARRIVED inside B3 Media's underground dock, its silent descent like a ghost. We disembarked quickly, slipping into the sleeping halls of the broadcast center. The air smelled of ozone and stale coffee, a place alive with signals and stories—a heart that pumped information to a waiting world.

Jadel eased Dom off his back, carefully settling him into a seat next to Ellen, my Dad, Yoshi, and me. Clustered around the control room, the glow of monitors reflected off our tense faces. Yoshi's fingers danced across the console, tying us into the global flex-link. Billions of connections flared to life, a mesh of light and data sparking with energetic potential, like neurons firing in the brain of a waking giant.

"It's live," Yoshi whispered.

I swallowed, the intensity of the moment pressing down on me. Julian Hollenbeck's figure coalesced into place on the largest screen—a hologram broadcast from Hollenbeck Media in the Aboves. His eyes burned with resolve and his jaw was set with unwavering determination.

"Citizens of Seneca. Citizens of Earth," he began…

The monitors split into a grid, each one showing a different newsfeed. Humanlike reporter bots stood poised in cities across the world, Julian's words flowing seamlessly from their mouths, translated into countless languages. The synchronization was eerie—a single message delivered through dozens of faces.

In Seneca, Becky Hudson stood on the steps of The Seneca Senate, her hair tucked behind her ears, her eyes wide with practiced sincerity. She spoke with the sincerity of the girl next door, the kind people trusted. "For too long, you have been living in a shadow—a shadow cast by two giants who have decided your future for you."

In Tokyo, a sleek, dark-haired bot with a soft lilt in her voice echoed the message in Japanese, her eyes reflecting the neon blur of Shibuya Crossing. "SGE Corp controls Doromium, the most powerful resource we have ever discovered. They hold it in their iron grip, promising progress while chaining us to their profit margins."

In São Paulo, a newsbot with warm brown eyes delivered the words in Portuguese, her tone rich with restrained fury "FlexCorp controls the technology— the implants in your bodies, the bots in your homes, the networks connecting your minds. They promise connection while they tighten the leash." In Lagos, a bot dressed in sharp professional attire spoke with passion. "Two empires, locked in a dance of mutual greed. Competing for power, yet feeding off each other's corruption. SGE fuels FlexCorp's machines. FlexCorp fuels SGE's domination."

The grid pulsed, a symphony of languages, each voice blending into a harmonious chorus of truth.

Julian's hologram on the main screen leaned forward, his eyes piercing. His voice rose, and the bots echoed him, a chorus of revolution. "They have carved up the future— a future where your autonomy, your choice, your very humanity are commodities to be bought and sold. But it does not have to be this way."

The air in B3 felt charged, like we were standing at the center of a lightning storm. My heart pounded in my chest. I could feel the network breathing, shifting, awakening.

"We stand on the edge of a new era," Julian continued. "Will we let these corporations chain us to their vision of the future? A future where we are nothing more than gears in their machine? Or will we rise together and reclaim what is ours— our resources, our technology, our destiny?"

The reporter bots spoke in unison now, their voices layered. The words poured like molten metal into the minds of billions.

"Knowledge is power, not manipulation and lies. They fear your understanding. They fear what you might do with the truth."

A tremor ran through me. The air was too still. The lights too bright. My gut clenched—like the world was holding its breath before a scream.

Julian's voice surged, raw and urgent. "We must release Doromium! The power belongs to the people!"

The bots repeated his call, eyes blazing with synthetic excitement. Becky Hudson's voice rang out across Seneca, clear and righteous. "The power belongs to *us*."

But even as the words filled the air, I tasted copper on my tongue. A cold prickle danced along my spine.

*No. Not yet. Not now.*

The screen showing Hollenbeck Media in the Aboves had an eerie static. The gleaming newsroom, the rows of monitors— and then the doors exploded inward. Dark figures swarmed in, weapons raised, faces obscured by helmets.

Julian turned toward the chaos, his eyes locking onto the camera, onto me.

"For everyone," he said.

A shot cracked. His body jerked. He crumpled to the floor.

The feed went to static.

The grid of reporter bots froze. The world held its

breath. In shock. Unsure. Then the screens darkened, the light collapsing in on itself.

The silence in B3 was absolute, an extension of Hollenbeck Media.

I couldn't breathe. My knees buckled. Dom's arm wrapped around me, holding himself upright. His body trembled, his breath ragged, the nanobots inside him warring for control.

The network surged with grief and rage, a billion minds reeling from the shock. But beneath the horror, something incredible was brewing.

Julian was gone. But his words—our truth—were alive.

The revolution had been televised.

Dom's voice was a whisper, tight with pain. "We did it."

Tears blurred my vision. My fingers curled into fists, the weight of grief and purpose intertwining.

# 31

B3'S TRANSMISSION still lingered in the air like the aftermath of a thunderstorm, a revelation too raw to be absorbed in silence. Screens blinked and fizzled with the remnants of Julian Hollenbeck's final message, his voice defiant even as it faded to static.

*"You are not passengers on this journey. You are the drivers. Take the wheel before it's too late."*

He had paid the price for that message. The price was his life. The cost would echo through our collective fabric forever. Ellen turned to me. "We're leaving," she said. "Your father and I will take charge of the Doromium release."

My dad nodded, his face lined with both worry and determination. "No matter what happens, I want you to know, this has always been for you."

"We'll see this through, Dad."

I swallowed hard, watching them disappear into the

hallway.

I turned back to the balcony in Hub 144, looking down through the double-sided glass that encased B3 Media into the chaos spilling into the hub's hallways below. The world was tearing at its seams—and the seams were made of lies. The gilded walls of the hub, once pristine, were shattering, jagged shards glinting like fractured light. Senecans picked up those shards, their hands bleeding, eyes blazing with fury and desperation.

The deep, resonant tremor beneath my feet was the signal: Lieutenant Otis's army had awakened. S.O.I.L. agents, their minds tethered to the cloud, moved with uncanny synchronization. Their eyes were void, stripped of humanity, bodies reduced to marionettes manipulated by code.

The hallways, once hopeful corridors of knowledge, had become battlegrounds. The golden splinters crunched underfoot, weapons born of destruction. People surged forward, their faces etched with a singular, relentless purpose: freedom.

I scanned the crowd, my breath caught in my throat. There—through the tangle of bodies—I saw my mom! She swung a shard of golden glass with a ferocity I had never seen, a warrior born of necessity. In that instant, the weight of all her secrets and sacrifices was laid bare.

With my heart hammering, I ran down into the crowd of Senecans, wanting to reach her—to fight by her side—but the air cracked. A pulse of electric energy screamed toward me. “Doro!”

Jadel's hand yanked me backward, a surge of deadly energy missing me by inches. I stumbled into Jadel’s chest, breathless, the scent of scorched air filling my lungs.

“You’re welcome,” he muttered, eyes wild but calm all in the same glance.

The battle was chaos incarnate. The agents fought with precision, but the Senecans fought with heart. The golden hallways peppered with dust and blood, the shards of their once-perfect world now weapons in their hands. I lost my mom in the crowd. The chaos blurred around me, and I knew the real battle was in the Cloud.

I closed my eyes and plunged inward, deep into the core of my consciousness where the lattice of synthetic intelligence lit up. Lieutenant Otis’s control was an uncanny dark pulse within the Cloud, radiating a smug certainty of assured victory.

"Not today," I spat through gritted teeth, diving deeper.

My consciousness became liquid light, flowing through the tangled pathways until I reached the heart of Lieutenant Otis’s puppeteering control. I wrapped my mental fingers around it, felt its resistance—slick, oily, desperate. He had fortified it well, but he hadn’t counted on me.

I inhaled a breath so deep it felt like I could swallow the world, then detonated my will inside it—a blast of pure, classic

Culver City rebellion. Lieutenant Otis's threads snapped like brittle vines. Control slipped from his grasp—and fell into mine. I gasped, the cloud intelligence shuddering as it shifted. S.O.I.L agents in the mob froze mid-motion, their eyes glazed over with confusion. The entire hub held its breath in awe.

With a surge of victory, I handed the reins over to Yoshi, hitting him up through flex:

*They're all yours, buddy.*

I knew Yoshi was on the other side of the glass, his fingers flying—a robotics wizard casting silent spells through the circuitry. He'd dismantle the bots' rhythm and rebuild it with a new destiny—the one we were fighting for.

The agents' eyes changed—the cold light replaced by a blank, waiting stillness. They were no longer FlexCorp's army. They were free agents now, human beings again, on the cusp of something new.

The tide was turning. The Senecans paused, weapons poised mid-strike, disbelief dawning on their faces. Then came the roar—a collective cry of victory. Strangers hugged, tears streamed, faces lifted to the shattered ceiling, revealing layers and layers of sectors and residences with Senecans pouring out in droves.

The collective intelligence was aligning with the truth we had unleashed. The Crystal Cloud was awake, aware, and angry. The crowd surged toward the Seneca Senate, a new manifesto blazing in their hearts—my dad's manifesto. The one stolen from him. Now, we were taking it back. In a world of machines, our spirit was the weapon they could never control. And now, it was unleashed.

# 32

THE GOLDEN HALLS of the Seneca Senate still shimmered with dust of the uprising. The dust was evidence that we had cracked open the illusion, but the piles still held pieces that were sharp and dangerous. We weren't done yet.

The chamber was filled to capacity, voices echoing off the high ceilings, vibrating with the sounds of dissonance. As I marched through the threshold to the heart of it all I was flanked by two people I never thought I'd march with: Brittany Gilroy and G.W. Wallingsford.

Each step we took forward carried the echo of their choices, choices that had torn them away from their powerful families and set them firmly on the side of truth. I glanced at them, and for a moment, the gravity of this alliance settled deep in my chest. These weren't just allies—they were symbols of what this revolution could be.

Ahead of us, the gilded Senate seats gleamed, filled with

senators and officials who had once dictated the fate of Seneca. Among them sat their fathers. Frank Wallingsford's face was a storm of disbelief and anger, his polished demeanor tarnished like silver. Senator Gilroy, however, looked calm, his eyes locked on his daughter. Neither man spoke, their silence brimming with tension.

We stopped at the base of the podium. Brittany and G.W. stood on one side of me, Dom on the other.

G.W. raised his hand, his voice fighting through the noise. "Today, we make things right," he shouted, glancing toward his father. "Not for legacy, not for power, but for all of us."

I saw Jennifer in the crowd give her brother an affirming nod.

To my side, Brittany also nodded. "I love Seneca. I always have." Her voice wavered for a moment before she steadied herself, her hands trembling near the microphone. "That's why I can't stay silent anymore. G.W. and I stand by Doro Campbell, and all of you. There is so much potential here, but we won't be ruled by greed or fear-based politics any longer. There is one person who has been fighting for all of us, and we want to introduce you to her now."

G.W. extended his hand towards the podium. "Doro, the Senate floor is yours."

Taking a deep breath, I stepped forward, the fragments

of shattered gold cracking softly underfoot. I looked to Dom. The last time we had been here we were on trial, but this was far different. His fierceness was back, breaking through his exhaustion with a vengeance, and it gave me even more power. "This is it, Doro," he said. "Time to show them that we're not just products of our past, but architects of our future."

All the senators leaned forward, some squirming, some with faces barely concealing apprehension. I met each senator's gaze, silently acknowledging their attention.

The crowd filled the vast underground chamber, their eyes wide with exhaustion and hope. And to my surprise, there, amidst the chaos, stood the one and only, Gregory Zaffron. He wasn't barking orders, wasn't sneering with authority. He stood shoulder-to-shoulder with his fellow Senecans, his gaze locked on mine. For once, he looked… humbly human.

A chant swelled, low and ragged at first. "Doro! Doro! Doro!" The sound of my name, carried on so many voices, sent a chill through me. They were calling on me—not just as a girl who fought back, but as someone who could lead them forward.

My fingers tightened around the manifesto my dad had given me—the glowing blueprint for a future worth believing in. My heart thundered in my chest as I stepped up to the podium Dom and I had once defended ourselves from, my boots crunching over fragments of debris and salt. I took a deep breath, tasting the true salt of the earth—our revolution. Our *evolution.*

"Look around you," I said, my voice trembling but steady. "These halls were built to shine. To impress. To remind us of who held the power. But today, we took that power back. Not with machines. Not with tech. But with our hearts, our minds, and our will to be free."

The crowd was silent, hanging on every word. I swallowed, feeling the truth rise inside me. "We live in a world where technology is used to control us, where stories are fed to us like poison, and we drink them down because it's easier than asking questions. But the truth is, we've been played. Manipulated. Lied to."

I saw heads nodding, fists pumping. They knew it. They'd felt it, too.

"But here's the thing about technology," I continued, lifting the manifesto high. "It isn't the enemy. Tech is just a mirror—it shows us what we decide to make. It's raw potential, powered by the human mind. And our minds? They don't have limits!"

A murmur rippled through the crowd.

"We are limitless! We don't have to choose between science and faith. Between progress and humanity. We can marry them. Because the one thing no machine can replicate is Consciousness. Self-awareness. The ability to look inside ourselves and ask: *Who am I? Why am I here? What can I do to make this world better?*"

I glanced at Dom, his eyes shining. At my mom, fierce and unbroken. My eyes swept over the crowd. Faces that had been part of my journey, part of me, came into focus. Dr. Cairncross met my gaze, her jaw set, eyes beaming with pride. She gave a single, intense nod that said more than any words could. All of this was her work, too.

Ty from Ty's Sushi stood just behind her, his ever-present bad-assery still intact. He gave a slight bow, a show of respect that made my breath catch. Some of my S.E.R.C. peers were scattered throughout the crowd, their eyes wide with a quiet determination that mirrored my own. Yoshi. McKayla, Brittany…

A swell of emotion rose in my throat. These weren't just faces in a crowd—they were people who had shaped my becoming, challenged me, believed in me even when I struggled to believe in myself. Each one felt like a piece of my story, a memory made flesh. Seeing them all here, standing shoulder to shoulder, it was like every moment of my life had led to this. I blinked hard, trying to steady myself.

The choices we'd made, the risks we'd taken—they weren't just for us. They were for everyone. We weren't just fragments of a broken world anymore. Together, we were the ones putting it back together. We were a force.

My voice cracked as it elevated. "We've been fed the lie that control equals safety. That obedience equals peace. But real peace—real freedom—comes from having the courage to create our own paths. To trust ourselves. To trust each other." I clutched and raised the illuminated manifesto in my hands.

"My father, Johnny Campbell, risked everything to give us this. A guide to a world where technology doesn't enslave us, but elevates us. Where knowledge is shared. Where freedom is protected!"

I took a breath and read the words aloud, my voice ringing through the cavernous space:

The Senecan Manifesto

- Doromium is hereby open source.
- Knowledge belongs to everyone.
- Every citizen is responsible for helping all the people of the planet, not just themselves.

  Because freedom isn't freedom if it's hoarded.
- Senecans shall pursue daily physical, mental, and spiritual growth.

  Because balance is strength.
- Seneca's technology and medicine will be shared with the Aboves.

  Because healing shouldn't be a privilege.
- Senecans will repopulate the Aboves, leading the shift forward.

  Because change starts with us.

- Senecans may travel freely between Seneca and the Aboves.

  Because walls divide; freedom unites.
- Separated loved ones may reunite.

  Because love is the truest freedom.

I looked up, my eyes stinging. The crowd was still, their faces open. "This isn't just a list of rules. It's a hard promise that we will never let fear control us again. That we will use our minds and our technology to heal—ourselves and our planet." I felt the words bubbling up from somewhere deep, deeper than fear, deeper than pain.

"The release of Doromium is coming. My father and Ellen Malone are making sure of that right now. And when it happens, it won't just heal the sky. It will be a symbol and reminder that we can rise above the lies. That we can be more. That we can be free." A wave of energy surged through the crowd. Tears glistened. Fists lifted.

"We stand on the edge of a new world. A world we're going to build together… and when that blue light fills the sky, remember this moment. Remember that *we* made it possible."

I stepped back, the roar of the crowd crashed over me like a tidal wave. Then, something even more powerful silenced us all. A hush so profound it felt as if the Earth itself was listening.

# 33

A TREMOR RAN through the ground beneath my feet, subtle yet undeniable, like the earth itself was about to let go after holding its breath. The air crackled with the charge of something massive and bubbling, its right to be unleashed.

A shiver drifted up my spine. This wasn't just the end of a fight—it was the edge of a precipice. We were teetering on the brink of something seismic. The crowd's eyes, wide and unblinking, reflected the same truth that was pulsing through my body.

Something was coming. Something vast, dynamic, and unstoppable. The Seneca Senate's underground chamber vibrated through the salt walls and into my bones. Light filtered from the colossal crystal chandeliers overhead, casting an ethereal illumination on the blue-robed senators who sat in hushed anticipation.

Beside me, Dom's hand tightened around mine, his grip

strong despite the weight of his exhaustion. We stood at two side-by-side podiums, surrounded by our peers, the rebels, the dreamers—those who refused to surrender to a future built on chains.

Among the sea of faces, Gregory Zaffron stood with his head bowed, not as the man who had once been our adversary, but as one who had chosen the side of truth. The shift in his demeanor surprised me, a quiet reassurance where I least expected it. I barely had time to process it before B3's broadcast burst to life.

Holographic screens flared above the Senate chamber, and a ripple of gasps echoed through the crowd. The rebel feeds streamed in, cascading like a futuristic river of truth. All around me, people tuned in—on their flexers, on floating FlexOculis. The world was watching, soaking it all up.

Julian Hollenbeck's voice crackled through the chamber, powerful and unbroken: *"You are not passengers on this journey. You are the drivers. Take the wheel before it's too late."*

I sat in my sympathy and gratitude for Teddy coming through, as the feeds broke into a mosaic of scenes:

In Culver City, my home, people gathered on street corners, rooftops, and in parks. Families, friends, neighbors—everyone watched as the sky began to shift. The familiar boulevards and palm-lined streets were bathed in an electric blue light. Faces turned upward, expressions of wonder showed up in places that had grown weary from years of concealment.

Across the world, golden ascension domes—hidden for too long beneath the earth—began to rise. The domes opened and Senecans emerged hesitantly, blinking against the brilliance of daylight, their faces pale and painted with awe. Trembling hands reached for the open air.

For the first time in years, they breathed the unfiltered air.

The rumble under my feet grew stronger, a heartbeat of the world itself. The images continued to pour in—pure liberation.

In Peru, the camera feeds shook with the force of revolution. Indigenous defenders celebrated, victorious in the rubble of the SGE Corp security posts. The ground below them quivered, and then—

A beam of pure blue light erupted from the earth.

It shot upward, a liquid column of Doromium energy, so vivid it felt like it could define reality itself. It was about to.

The blue light poured into the heavens, a blazing stream of sapphire brilliance. It rose higher and higher, a spear piercing the celestial atmosphere, refracting through the clouds in chains of luminescent fireworks.

The Senate chamber was bathed in the glow of the broadcast. The golden carvings of the two hundred and twelve senators illuminated with new life, their stoic faces cast in hues of blue from the broadcasts.

I turned to Dom. The electric glow brought his eyes back to life, chasing away the shadows of invasion.

"It's happening," he whispered, his voice catching.

I nodded, tears streaming freely now.

The Doromium beam pulsed brighter, spreading across the sky like liquid. Cracks in the sky melted away, the air stretching gently into tranquility like low tide at Leo Carrillo State Beach.

The broadcasts showed people falling to their knees, hands pressed to the ground, faces lifted to the sky in awe. Strangers embraced, tears mixing with laughter. The world—our world—was changing before our very eyes.

In research labs and environmental sanctuaries, scientists were already mobilizing, stepping forward to safeguard this new energy, nurture Doromium responsibly, and ensure its power would never again be harnessed for control. The energy of the revolution was theirs to guide, not exploit.

In Los Angeles, I saw kids riding their bikes down streets that hadn't felt safe in years. Parents held their children up to the light, whispering prayers of thanks.

The Doromium beam surged one final time, a crescendo of light that seemed to stitch the world back together. Then, like a sigh, it faded, absorbed into the atmosphere it was working to heal. The blue veil settled into the sky.

The broadcasts tuned out, leaving behind a stillness so sweet it felt like the earth itself had paused to take a breath.

Around me, the crowd stood in silence, tears streaming down faces filled with wonder, exhaustion, and hope. The fight was brutal but worth it. We had unleashed something they could never cage. We had unleashed hope.

# 34

EVERY BREATH HELD in collective suspension as we stood on the precipice of change, one step from tipping the world on its axis. My mom stepped forward. The burnished light of the Seneca Senate illuminated her face—the same face I'd seen bent over breakfast plates, bandaging scraped knees, and holding everything together when life was falling apart. But there was something new in her eyes.

"I need you all to listen carefully," she said, her voice clear as glass. "FlexCorp and SGE Corp have one last fail-safe embedded in the Crystal Cloud. A kill switch they think will end this revolution. But they have underestimated you."

A murmur passed through the crowd, confusion and curiosity mingling. I felt it, too, the buzz of disbelief cracking through my own understanding.

Gregory Zaffron's voice cut through the silence. "Nora, you've been one of us this whole time?"

She turned to him, her chin lifting. "Not just one of you."

A voice boomed from the back of the crowd, dripping with disdain. "Enough!"

Lieutenant Marcus Otis stepped forward from the shadows, fury in his eyes. His uniform was disheveled, his confidence fraying at the edges. The silence in the room shattered as Lieutenant Otis raised his arm, a sleek, metallic device strapped to his forearm, glowing with pulsating veins of electric blue. The vibration it emitted was low and insidious, and it made my teeth ache.

People stumbled back, hands clutching their temples, eyes wide with panic. I knew that sound—a Sonic Disruption Cannon. One wrong move, and he could reduce this assembly to a mass of incapacitated bodies… or worse.

Lieutenant Otis's lips curled into a snarl. "One step out of line, and I'll make sure you never take another."

The invisible pressure pushed against our skulls. The threat wasn't just real—it was seconds from becoming lethal. His hand trembled with barely suppressed rage. "You think your little rebellion can rewrite the world?"

He turned his gaze on my mom, then me. "This ends here, Nora *and child*."

But before he could act, a group of S.O.I.L. guards surged forward. Their eyes, once vacant under Lieutenant Otis's control, now alive—charged with the fury of millions. They moved as one, weapons aimed not at us, but at him.

"Lieutenant Marcus Otis," one of the guards said, his voice resolute, "you are under arrest for crimes against humanity."

Lieutenant Otis's eyes widened, the realization smacking him in the face. His power was gone. He took a step back, his control crumbling into desperation.

"You can't do this!" he spat. "I gave you orders! I—" The guards seized his arms, pulling him down to his knees. I caught my mom's eye, and for a moment, we both understood: the old world was collapsing, piece-by-piece. Lieutenant Otis's cries faded as the guards dragged him away, his power dissolving into nothing. A collective exhale swept through the crowd. All eyes turned to my mom, demanding answers.

She stepped forward, her shoulders straight.

"I know you all need more answers than I can give but there is something I can share. Before I was Layla Campbell, I was Special Agent Nora Shehadeh. My husband and I left that life when Doro was born. We wanted a normal life for her. I became an occupational health nurse for the agency, traveling wherever Johnny was stationed. We settled in Southern California—my home—when Johnny moved to the private sector. That's when he discovered Doromium."

I sucked in a breath. Pieces of my life clicked into place

like tumblers in a lock. My dad's distant gazes, my mom's trips for "conferences," all the locked doors in our home.

My mom's voice softened, eyes glimmering with memories. "He told me he left the secret life behind. But when they offered him a chance to come back, he couldn't say no. I didn't ask questions. And when he disappeared... I fell apart. I believed he was on an assignment, but I had no answers. When Ellen showed up, recruiting Doro to a 'boarding school,' I knew it was tied to Johnny. That's why I let her go."

Her hand drifted to her necklace, fingers brushing against a pendant that had always been there—a subtle piece of jewelry. Dm. Doromium. The realization seared through me. The same symbol had been on Ellen's lapel the day she came for me. And Jadel's in the jungle. My mom had known. She had let me go, trusting in something greater, something unspoken between the lines of our lives.

I blinked away the sting in my eyes. "You knew this whole time?" My voice trembled.

She nodded, her gaze holding mine. "I knew you were meant for something bigger. I didn't want to lose you, but I knew I had to trust you."

The weight of her sacrifice settled on me, a mantle of love and faith that stretched beyond understanding. There was no time to unravel it all now, but I had to let my mom know. "I know why you kept things hidden. You were doing what you thought was best. You were trying to protect me. But you were preparing me for this and you didn't even know it."

Just then, the answer flashed in my mind. "The fail-safe is in the Crystal Cloud," I said, the words falling into place. "We need a direct connection to take it down. A Neural Link—between us… and Dad!"

My mom's eyes glowed with fierce pride.

I continued, "The Crystal Cloud needs to have Dad's knowledge and control of Doromium. Because then it will truly belong to the people. It's the only way."

The crowd parted, Seneca leaders stepping back. I took a breath that seemed to pull the universe inside me. My fingers danced over the console, weaving pathways of quantum data, threading a bridge that ignored distance and defied reality.

The Neural Link flared, a torrent of data surging through the conduit. The fail-safe writhed in the Crystal Cloud, a dark pulse of corrupted code—slippery, elusive.

Dom's hand tightened around mine. His eyes, though bloodshot were filled with rapids of information.

"Doro, listen. The fail-safe… it's adaptive, like a neural net. It's learning how to resist us." His voice was ragged, but his eyes sharpened. "I worked with adaptive feedback loops tracking whale migration patterns. The fail-safe is learning our moves the same way—but we can trick it."

My heart pounded. "How?!"

He drew a shaky breath, his fingers trembling. "Remember when you used the quantum feedback loop in Peru?"

Oh. My. Gosh. Yes! "I can mirror its signals back on itself—overwhelm it. It won't know what's real. It'll collapse under its own contradictions."

A spark of recognition ignited in my mind. Quantum feedback loops—the same principle that allowed researchers to track whales by bouncing entangled signals off their neural patterns. If we could create a mirrored loop in the Cloud, the fail-safe's adaptive defenses would fold in on themselves, unable to process the conflicting data.

I squeezed his hand. "You're brilliant."

The chamber dimmed as the connection solidified, a column of light erupting between us—a swirling vortex of gold and Seneca blue.

Then, my dad appeared. Johnny Campbell flickered into being right in front of us, a radiant projection of light and memory. The brilliance expanded, fluid and alive, until it reached my mom… and the two of them walked towards each other.

The moment the light touched her, it didn't just encircle her—it recognized her, as if completing a circuit long broken. They stood together, bound by more than technology, more than time. It was as though the universe itself exhaled, bridging the distance between presence and absence, flesh and light.

They faced each other across the light, the distance between them alive with a power that defied explanation. They lifted their hands, fingertips nearly touching. Sparks snapped and hissed between them, arcs of energy vibrating in the air. The static charged the room, lifting the hair on my arms, raising goosebumps on my skin. Everyone could feel it —the raw, undiluted force of connection, a love that transcended separation, time, and space. And in that charged stillness, something inside me clicked into place. For the first time since I was a little girl, I felt whole again.

My mom's eyes were filled with a life I had not seen in years. "Johnny, it's time to end this."

He met her intensity, unwavering—all in. "Let's close this chapter."

"So we can write a new one," she said.

Their eyes held steady, igniting all the sparks they needed right then and there… and the neural link flared, a torrent of data surging through the conduit. Our minds synced, a trinity of purpose. My mother's intelligence, my father's ingenuity, and my own resolve wove together. I could see the fail-safe now—a dark pulse writhing in the Crystal Cloud like a parasite. It resisted, twisted, but we were relentless.

"Now!" I shouted.

We plunged our will into the heart of the fail-safe,

detonating it with a supernova of intention. The black pulse shattered, dissolving into nothing. The Crystal Cloud was purified, reclaimed by the people it was meant to serve.

The light dimmed, my parents' holograms flickering. They reached for each other, hands still hovering, the energy between them electric and alive. The room erupted in cheers, a roar of victory and release.

# 35

THE MORNING AFTER the release of Doromium, the world felt like it was finally waking up. As I scrolled through the feeds on the B3 channel, it wasn't through the lens of S.O.I.L. or any corporation's influence anymore. Becky Hudson, the face of fabricated news, was toast. This was *Julian Hollenbeck's dream realized*—unfiltered, uncorrupted truth, delivered by the people, for the people. He hadn't lost his life in vain. His belief in the power of an honest story was alive, moving through millions of voices.

I glanced around my half-packed residence, preparing to return to the Aboves. The urge to leave was tempered by the scenes unfolding on my screen. The downfall was happening in real time, and I *needed* to witness it.

Northern Virginia's corporate skyline sprawled across the displays—buildings that once loomed like untouchable monuments of power. But not today. FlexCorp Headquarters stood rigid and unyielding, a glass-and-steel fortress now ringed with swirling red and blue lights. Federal agents stormed through the lobby doors. Servers were being seized, hidden information dragged into the light.

The feed shifted to another location—a sleek, angular structure tucked into a wooded expanse by the secretive waters of Claytor Lake. SGE Corp.'s headquarters looked almost serene, but the calm was a facade. Black vehicles lined the perimeter. This was the place where S.O.I.L. agents once tracked our every move, where the mainframe held the entangled minds of Senecans. Now, it was exposed—laid bare for the world to see

A black convoy glided to a halt in front of the courthouse, cameras flashing in staccato bursts. Journalists' voices elevated in a chaotic crescendo of questions. The doors swung open, and figures emerged, their expressions carefully blank. Executives who once dictated lives with the push of a button, were now the defendants, their power dissolved under the relentless weight of justice.

The crowd surged forward with an unrelenting barrage of questions for the former titans of FlexCorp and SGE Corp, including none other than Billy Wallingsford. They shuffled up the courthouse steps, their carefully curated masks cracking under the pressure of exposure. The once-powerful, now just *people*, stripped of their facades.

I powered down my screens. I'd seen enough for now

and felt comforted in knowing that justice was unfolding.

Just as I turned away, the soft chime of the doorbell rang. Curious, I waved my hand over the door console. The panel slid open with a whisper, revealing not one person, but three: my mom, Ellen, and Richmond Shields. They stood there in an awkward triangle, each of them looking slightly surprised to see the others. I crossed my arms with a smirk across my face. “Did you all come together?”

Ellen shook her head with a wry smile. “I thought I was the only one.”

My mom tilted her head. “Trust me, this reunion wasn’t on my agenda either.”

Professor Shields cleared his throat, his eyes glinting with amusement. “I was just coming to give you your final grade before you headed off for new endeavors.”

I stepped aside, letting them in. The door panel whispered closed behind them, sealing us in the quiet cocoon of my residence. For a moment, no one spoke.

My mom broke the silence first. She turned to Ellen. “Thank you, Ellen. For protecting Doro. For believing in her when I didn’t understand the full extent of what she needed.”

Ellen’s eyes softened. “You gave her the courage to take the first step.”

After a moment of silent gratitude, Shields’s eyes met Ellen’s. “Ready to get back to work, Malone?”

Her lips lifted into a faint smile. “Always.”

The look they exchanged held the a spark of something just beginning. I didn’t miss it—and neither did my mom. She arched an eyebrow, but said nothing.

I took a breath, steadying the anticipation rising in my chest. I had something else to do. Something that I had waited a long time for.

# 36

THE AIR IN Washington, D.C. tasted different now—lighter, warmer, tinged with a hint of melted butter and toasted bread. The sky was a perfect wash of cornflower blue, the kind that made you believe in new beginnings.

I leaned against the counter of the grilled cheese stand, the scent of sizzling cheese mingling with the faint aroma of blooming cherry blossoms. Around us, the city had awoken with life and a new rhythm that felt... harmonious. As if the gears of transition had finally stopped grinding and clicked into place.

A line of food flighters hugged the edge of the National Mall, where the towering white monuments didn't feel like relics in this moment. They felt like markers of a place waking up, stretching its limbs, and remembering what it was supposed to be. Kids chased each other across the lawn by the reflection pool, their laughter carried by the breeze. Street musicians played riffs on upside-down buckets that rippled out like invitations to dance.

Reba grinned at the stand's menu, his eyes scanning the options. "They've got twelve types of grilled cheese. *Twelve.* How's anyone supposed to choose?"

"Just get all of them," I said, elbowing him. "You've earned it."

His laughter rang out, unfiltered. The kind of laugh that reminded you of what freedom sounded like.

The stand's owner, a woman with a gap-toothed smile and a tattoo of a cow with wings, slid two crisp and golden sandwiches across the counter. "You two look like you could use the extra-crispy special. Melty in the middle, crunchy on the edges."

"Perfect," Reba said, scanning his flexer to pay.

We took our sandwiches and wandered a few steps away. Across the street, the new Intuerian Institute gleamed with smooth curves and walls that seemed to breathe with the light. The sign above the entrance was simple and unassuming: *The Intuerian Institute for Insight and Understanding.*

"Your name's going to be on a plaque in there," I said, taking a bite. The cheese stretched, warm and gooey, a taste of comfort I hadn't realized I missed.

Reba shook his head, a soft smile playing on his lips. "It's not about the plaque. It's about what it means. People are finally seeing us—understanding us. Intuerians don't have to hide anymore."

A breeze picked up, rustling the banners hanging from lampposts. They weren't filled with political slogans or corporate logos. They were stamped with simple, powerful words: *Empathy. Insight. Evolution.*

Reba's eyes were fixed on the Institute's entrance, where a small crowd was gathered. Some held signs welcoming the change. A few carried flowers, a silent offering of respect. No fear. No suspicion. Just... acceptance.

I took a deep breath. "Hey, Reebs?"

He turned to me, mid-bite, eyebrows raised.

"Yeah?"

I smiled, slow and secretive. "I have a surprise for you."

He blinked, confused. "A surprise? For me?"

I nodded toward the path leading up to the Institute.

He followed my eye-line—and froze.

Lindsay stood there, framed by the sunlight, her dark curls lifting gently in the breeze. She wore a simple jacket, her eyes scanning the crowd, searching. Her expression hovered between exhilaration and hesitation, like she wasn't sure if this moment was real. Reba's long-lost girlfriend, his first love. In the midst of the interconnectedness of the Crystal Cloud, I had found her, and knew I had to reunite them.

Reba's grilled cheese slipped from his fingers, landing forgotten on the grass. His eyes went wide, his breath catching in his throat.

"No way," he said, his voice barely audible. "How did I not see this coming?"

I grinned, my chest tightening with joy. "Guess even Intuerians can be surprised."

He looked at me, stunned. "You... Doro, you did this?"

"Yeah," I said softly. "Because some things aren't meant to be seen in advance. Some things are meant to just... happen."

He swallowed, his eyes beaming. For a moment, he didn't move. And then he did, his feet carrying him forward like he was being pulled by a force stronger than logic.

"Lindsay?" he called out, his voice cracking.

She turned at the sound of her name, her eyes locking onto his. Everything else fell away—the city, the people, the noise.

"Timothy," she whispered.

He closed the distance in three strides, his arms wrapping around her, hugging her and lifting her off the ground like he was afraid she might disappear. Her fingers clutched at his oversized hoodie, her eyes squeezing shut as tears slipped down her cheeks.

"I never thought I would see you again," she choked out. He pulled back just enough to look into her eyes, his own face open, vulnerable. "I know. And I am so, so sorry." They embraced, the space between them dissolving, the years of separation folding in on them. The air seemed to buzz, not with technology, but with something deeper—something that didn't need explanation.

I watched, my heart full. This was the power of love. The power of mystery. Some connections couldn't be calculated or predicted. They simply were. Reba turned back to me, his eyes bright, his gentle smile appearing. "Thank you, Campbella." I shrugged, my own smile breaking free. "You deserved a happy surprise."

He laughed, took Lindsay's hand, and turned toward the Institute. "Come with me, I want to show you my new gig. And I hope you'll stick around for a while."

# 37

I ARRIVED ON Coconut Island in Hawaii. The winds whispered through the palm trees, brushing salt-sweetened air across my face. This place felt like an old memory reborn—a world not dictated by lines of code or the sizzle of grids and processors, but by the randomized rhythmic pulse of gentle waves meeting the Palomino colored sand. The universe condensed here, into the simple symmetry of beach, wind, and sky. Eternal truths to embrace, not data points to manipulate. I felt at home.

My eyes fell on Dom, his figure silhouetted against the fading embers of the sun on the steadfast horizon. His presence was no different— even in his darkest hours he was a rock for me. The choice before me— to follow Seneca's interplanetary migration to Mars or stay on Earth— wasn't a calculation or algorithm to solve. It was a whisper from the observer within, the part of me that had been here all along. A whisper that rose from a place beyond intellect, beyond logic.

He didn't notice that I'd arrived, so I watched him, in awe of his brilliance. He guided a cluster of small, luminescent holo-drones that hovered just above the water's surface. The drones pulsed with faint blue and green lights, mapping the ocean floor and communicating with swarms of microscopic aquatic nanobots below.

Dom had followed his whisper to this peaceful island, refocusing his purpose—restoring marine biology from the heart of one of Earth's most treasured sanctuaries. To see him like this, fully in his element, was a gift. I realized that all I'd ever seen before was how he'd been robbed of that.

"Woof, woof, woof!"

Killer charged toward Dom. Dom spun around, his eyes catching the last streaks of gold in the sky as he scooped up the little dog.

"Killer!" he laughed.

Then his smile widened, genuine and unguarded. "Doro! I thought you were coming tomorrow!"

"I caught the last flight out of National," I said, my own smile breaking free. "I couldn't wait another night."

"Look at this!" he said, his voice thick with excitement.

"The reef's starting to rebuild itself! The nanobots are replicating the calcium carbonate structures, and the algae are thriving again."

I joined him at the water's edge, the waves lapping

gently at our feet. His technology didn't force nature to comply; it partnered with it, a reminder that the best innovations come from respect, not dominance. "I am so proud of you," I whispered into his ear as I kissed his neck.

His fingers brushed a stray strand of hair from my cheek. His touch lingered, his eyes meeting mine. "Do you know," he said softly, "how long I've been waiting for this? Just... us."

I smiled, my breath catching as his hand rested near my chin. "And Killer," I added.

We both laughed.

"I've been waiting a long time for this, too." I replied. "Since the first time I saw you in S.E.R.C. and you wanted nothing to do with me."

"Ha! Hardly!"

Dom and I stood at the edge of the Pacific together, the gentle crash of waves. The rolling expanse of endless motion in front of us was wild and untamed. It was everything the dam at Claytor Lake wasn't. I closed my eyes, remembering the lake— still, trapped, its waters held back by walls of concrete. The dam controlled the flow, forcing the water to serve, to be measured, contained, siphoned off for power. Energy, stolen and caged.

The ocean here was different. There were no barriers, no boundaries. The waves moved with their own rhythm, surging and retreating— a motion older than any civilization. The water didn't ask permission to exist or expand; it simply *was*, limitless and alive.

The damage SGE Corporation had done at Claytor Lake felt like a distant echo now, no longer a threat to our existence. The dam's grip on Dom's mind— on his purpose— had crumbled. The containment was gone, and the currents of the Pacific were pulling him forward.

For the first time in what felt like forever, Dom *was* the ocean. Boundless. Whole. He tilted his head, his eyes darkening with something that made my skin tingle. His voice was low, edged with warmth. "No more saving the world tonight, Doro Campbell."

"No more saving the world," I agreed, a laugh escaping me. The sound was light and strange in its unfamiliarity.

Dom leaned in slowly, giving us time to take in every detail of the moment and savor this. Just us. His lips brushed mine, tentative at first, then deeper. The world narrowed to the warmth of his mouth, the faint salt of the sea on his skin. My heart fluttered, not out of fear or adrenaline, but because I wasn't calculating outcomes. I was just feeling.

When we parted, he leaned back in and rested his forehead against mine. His fingers traced a pattern of a heart on my wrist.

"You're staying, aren't you?"

I exhaled, the truth settling in my bones. "Where else would I go?"

He didn't need to say anything more. He pulled me close, and we stood there, wrapped in each other. The world reduced to the sound of waves, Killer panting, and the calm feeling of our heartbeats together. For once, it didn't matter what lay beyond the sky or beneath the surface of things.

The kaleidoscopic synthesis of thoughts, feelings, energies, and experiences swirled inside me. Up until these days, I'd clamored for facts and answers, believing they were the key to my purpose. But that pursuit had only left me wanting more. When I loosened my grasp on the need for answers, the fog faded, and the light burst all around. The observer in me—the naked *I*—took its rightful place.

I thought of Reba, his glow lighting the way as he led me through the hazy, in-between spaces of my mind, showing me the delicate threads binding every life to each other. His journey to reconnect with Lindsay, a reminder that even destruction could give way to new beginnings.

Broken systems and relationships were healing, evolving. Technology had once been my obsession—a tool to dominate, to break systems wide open. My curiosity was once solely dominated by an insatiable hunger for advancing technologies to invade global computerized systems and algorithms for the thrill of it. I remembered the millions I'd funneled away, the cold satisfaction of stacking chips in my account. I hadn't seen the faces behind the losses. I hadn't thought about Fatima, the girl whose life was shattered by a father drowning in gambling debt. My shoulders had been heavy with the weight of that suffering.

Now that weight was transformed. When I woke up on that table in C-QNCE, I was given another chance to do what I was meant to do here. Time was a gift as long as it was in my hands, and only after spending it and learning hard lessons could I arrive where I was meant to be. My path had diverged from destruction to creation. From tearing down flawed systems to building new ones rooted in connection and growth.

Creating bigger, badder, and faster machines would always be a crucial part of our intellectual evolution, yes, but how naïve would I be to continue believing those technologies would save us? This wasn't just about how many trillions of light-years away we can erect habitats for our species. What about how far we take ourselves within?

As humanity hurtled toward new frontiers, evolving to survive on intergalactic soil, I saw the immense potential of our technology. Tools to heal, to build, to understand our genetic fabric, to stretch the boundaries of our existence. But even in those advancements, I knew a fundamental truth: technology couldn't save us from ourselves. It could be a conduit to breakthroughs, or it could be our undoing. The choice was ours.

So, who were we, beneath the machines? How did we want to live, to treat each other, to inhabit our own hearts and souls? The answers didn't lie in the mechanics of things but in the unseen spirit that connected us—the same spirit we neglected when we neglected our planet.

The Hawaiian sand was cool beneath my feet, grounding me more deeply than any metal spacecraft ever could. As we said "aloha" to the night sky, I reached for Dom's hand, his fingers closing around mine, warm and solid. I had my answer. Not an escape to the stars beginning to twinkle above me, but a commitment to the imperfect, beautiful chaos of Earth. To the quiet work of rebuilding, healing, and loving what was right in front of me.

The future stretched ahead, a boundless space of unknowns. I saw Mars, red and unyielding, a frontier of genetic adaptation and technological marvels. But I also saw Earth, scarred and breathtaking, its people—*my* people, with a desire for more than survival. A chance to reconnect, to evolve inward as well as outward.

I smiled, eyes wide open, trusting the journey. Trusting the endless dance of light and shadow. Trusting the infinite universe within us and beyond. This—here, now—was where the real adventure began.

# *Epilogue*

LOS ANGELES WAS bathed in a silky light that felt like forgiveness. The air was clean—the kind of clean that filled your lungs without the sting of radiation or the suffocation of masks and suits. People walked the streets, faces upturned, eyes squinting into a sky filled with peace, not pain.

I leaned against the door of my flighter, in front of Culver City High. The bell rang, and a stream of students poured out, their laughter and chatter swirling into the warm breeze.

Mr. Malin stepped outside, his eyes landing on me with that familiar twinkle. "See," he said, grinning. "I knew you weren't just going to skate by as a C student."

I shrugged, a smile breaking free. "I guess sometimes we get caught up in what we *don't* want, and it keeps us from doing what we *do* want."

"And now?" he asked.

I nodded toward the doors. "I'm here to pick up my friend."

Julie burst through the doors, her eyes lighting up when

she saw me. Without missing a beat, she dove into the passenger seat, her grin full of mischief—the same grin that once got us both busted.

"Doromium," she said with a smirk as her automated seatbelt snapped into place. "How did I not think of that?"

I grinned right back at my best friend, fingers grazing the controls. The console pulsed softly under my touch, the engine humming with barely-contained energy. No alarms blared. No security drones chased us. We were legit—legally in control of a fighter-class flighter. Who'd have thought?

"Ready?" I asked, daring the universe.

Julie's smile widened. Without a word, I punched the throttle. The flighter surged, lifting off with the grace of a feather and the power of a rocket. The asphalt fell away, and the city revealed itself beneath us—clear, alive, and smog-free.

The Pacific stretched out, a sapphire blanket meeting the endless curve of a baby-blue sky. We climbed higher, the world shrinking to a mosaic of memories and possibility.

I glanced at Julie. Her hair whipped around her face. "Where to?" she asked.

"Wherever we want!"

As we soared over the clear skies of Los Angeles, I imagined Ellen and Professor Shields looking out over Mars which was no longer a distant dream. It was a promise—a new canvas where humanity could paint with everything we'd learned.

Our flighter carved a path through the open blue, leaving nothing behind but a ripple of air and the promise of everything ahead. It was summertime in Los Angeles, and for the first time, the future wasn't a puzzle to solve. We were reaching inward to heal Earth, and outward to explore the stars. Both paths mattered. Both paths were *ours*.

## Acknowledgments

Little did I know, when the idea for Seneca sparked in my mind in 2013, it would grow to take on a life of its own. Here we are, twelve years and almost two hundred thousand words later, and here are the people I thank for helping me do this:

My mom, Ellen—your generosity of love and spirit. Your unparalleled patience. It's no wonder so many people say, "I love your mom!" Mom, you are pure love and that is what it is all about. Also, thank you for making me look good with legit grammar throughout this series and my whole life.

My husband, Aaron—this time-traveling adventure we're on is the greatest blessing. I could not have created the story of Seneca without you, not in a million years. It only took us a conversation that lasted over a decade. I'll never forget when you wrote to me, "You put the art in heart." Perfect because you are the "he" with whom "art" completes my heart.

London—your creativity, your voracious reading, love of animals, music, and art! I hope you will always find within these pages the inspiration to look inside yourself for every gift you will ever need to live a life filled with love and courage in a tough and rigid world. What's outside of you will always challenge and test you, but you are so powerful. Keep diving deep to understand what it means to be present and to lead with love.

Simone—your spunk, your bold and outgoing nature, your fierce loyalty, boundless Christmas spirit, and deep sense of empathy for those you love! It lights me up to see you enthralled by stories, and I hope that when you are old enough to read these books, you'll realize all these words are for you. Please always trust in yourself and your intuition, and remember that despite the bad out there, what you choose to give to the world can and will forever impact it for the better.

My family—from my sisters to my mom's cousin, Annabel Clark, who kept urging me to continue Doro's story.

My dear friends who have supported me over the years with refining these pages through edits, notes, creative direction, and invaluable insights—Behnam Karbassi, Marcus Lee, Magnus Kim, Justin Brimmer, Claudette Sutherland, Michael Shields, Chris Thompson, Charlotte Kruse, Miss Anonymous, Steve Peters and Chris Tomasino. I may have written the words, but because of you I have been able to bring this dream to reality; from the book itself to the transmedia experience and photography. Each one of you who contributed to carving this Senecan path at some point along the way, thank you.

Fallon Ureda—thank you for not only jumping in during *Element,* but also for fully embedding yourself in the story, ensuring that this complex narrative flows seamlessly. And thank you for loving it. And for not letting me start too many sentences with "and".

My tennis community, friends and *The Monarchs*—You gave me balance and a healthy outlet that, while momentarily distracting me from finishing this book (and everything else in life haha), ultimately enhanced my life in ways that challenged and elevated me as an individual, a teammate, and—at 47 years old, I can say with confidence—an athlete.

My coaches—Vedant & Jess. Vedant, you gave me the tools and tweaks to grow into a solid tennis player. Your dedication and tennis IQ are mind-blowing—thank you for sharing them with me.

Jess Browne—You helped me conquer my fear of "the hot seat"

and developed my game in ways I never imagined possible. I cherish the gift of your friendship that we've grown in the process. It's been a freaking blast. Thank you.

My support came from far and wide—from Lisa Keatts' 5th grade classes, who let me come in to talk about story and character with them, to the Barnes & Noble in Thousand Oaks, who hosted my first book signing. To the book bloggers and reviewers who took the time to dive into my story and spread the word—thank you all so very much.

After the release of *Seneca Element*, an old friend said to me, "Your dad would be so proud." That comment has always stayed with me. My dad, Shukri Gabriel Deeb, was an artist, a visionary, and a gentle soul who took the road less traveled. He endured incredibly deep pain and suffering in his lifetime, but never quit. The way he approached his work and art, and how he merged the two, instilled in me the belief that I could pursue my dreams. Not a day goes by that my Baba isn't missed, or that I don't wish he had gotten to know his granddaughters and they could have know him. When I tell them stories about him, I am reminded that, even though we may see our lives come and go in the blink of an eye, the impact we have lasts far beyond our time here. In many ways, that is what *Seneca* is about.

Thank you.

Rayya Deeb is a mother, wife, writer and Virginia Tech Hokie, born in London, England and raised in Northern Virginia. Seneca Evolution is her third novel. She lives in Southern California with her husband, two daughters & sweet dog. Visit her at www.rayyadeeb.com

Printed in Dunstable, United Kingdom